The Girl Mechanic of Wanzhou

Marjorie Sayer

Author's Note

Wanzhou is a fictional city. It is modeled after several large cities situated on the Grand Canal in China.

Two historical Chinese poems quoted in the text were translated by Alan Liu and Marjorie Sayer: Letter to Lady Tao Qiu by Qiu Jin, 1907, and River Snow by Liu Zong Yang, 813 (Tang Dynasty).

Copyright © 2012 Marjorie Sayer, Atelier Finwhale

All rights reserved.

Cover design and illustration by Dwenbon Kak-Volk.

ISBN: 149291990X
ISBN-13: 978-1492919902

For Alan, Miranda, Ava

1. The Last Ride Home

Wanzhou, China, October 1902

The last afternoon of her father's life, Zun watched a metal mold filled with brown sand. She was so excited to see the cast come out she couldn't do anything else. She loved it at the foundry: the resonant clang of hammers in the forge, the shower of sparks, the hot metal smell that pushed against her face. It was tricky – alloying iron. The slightest exposure to air would contaminate it. She and Ba had carefully flooded the melting chamber with inert gas. At last Ba upended the mold on a tray, and scraped the mound of sand with a brush. Curved grey metal emerged like the carapace of an enormous insect. It was a steel cylinder for a steam engine.

Zun didn't say a word as her father picked it up with tongs. She understood he had to concentrate. The man who came to watch them had no such reservations.

The foundry owner, Pang, was a jowly man in his fifties with an olive-sized cheek mole. He made the same joke whenever he saw Zun.

"My young bride is here! How happy I'll be when you ride through my gate in your red silk dress. Ha, ha!"

"Ba, I think the argon hood worked properly this time," Zun said loudly. "It kept out *corrosive vapors*." She glared at Pang.

"Listen to her! How cute! Of course, once she has a baby, she'll forget about metal," said Pang.

I'm twelve years old! What would I do with a baby? Zun raged inside. She blurted, "Pang Laoban, you are absolutely – "

"Zun, the cast is cool enough. It's time to go," said Ba. "Now."

Pang's chuckle rattled in Zun's ears, but she silently followed her father to the exit.

They left the foundry on the Phoenix, a French bicycle Ba had brought from Shanghai. Ordinary bicycles were as tall as a man, with a huge front wheel. The Phoenix had two wheels the same size, just under half Ba's height. It coasted with a soft ticking sound. When Zun sat on the bicycle crossbar between his arms, she felt invisible and loved it. As they wove amid the crowd on Wanzhou's canal-lined streets, no one noticed *her*; people stared at the bicycle – a twentieth-century marvel – and waved and called out to Ba, who waved and called back. Zun could see, unseen.

A man pulled a cart, sinewy calves pulsing along the street. A bobbing ox head dribbled flecks of foam. A little boy parted cracked lips to cry. A woman squatted to feed a fire, its orange flames cold, like the dying rays of the afternoon sun that failed to warm the October air.

Zun knifed her nose up at her father. "Ba, will you please tell Pang, *no more* bride jokes?"

"He means it as a compliment, you know."

"No, he doesn't. He knows I hate it. If he can't tell, he's blind. Let him save his compliments for his wives."

"That's how men like him talk. A girl is as good as she's able to marry, and Pang is quite a catch. It's his way of showing respect to you, believe it or not."

"As if I'll marry anyone!"

"I thought we agreed on nine grandchildren. Minimum," said Ba.

Big joke. He didn't understand. She couldn't explain her dread at Pang's teasing.

"Ma says getting married means you put on your husband's troubles, like a four-hundred-pound coat."

"How that woman exaggerates! Mine is three hundred pounds, at most." Ba paused. "Well, you know I have to be on good terms with Pang. He has the only blast furnace in town. I'm meeting him tomorrow, but you can stay home."

"Ba, you can't mean that."

"Old Liu One-Eye is a good guy. You can watch him work at the forge. No need to set foot in Pang's office."

So that was Ba's solution – a one-eyed nanny. Her least favorite thought bubbled up in her mind: *it would all be different if I were a boy*. She hated that thought, because she wasn't a boy, end of story. It seemed to come up more and more often – ever since she shot up in height, her eyes the level of Ba's chin.

"What are you and Pang going to talk about?"

"Hold on!" The bicycle skirted some ducks. Ba dodged one pothole but bumped into another. Zun nearly fell off.

Ba put a foot down to stop the bicycle from falling. Then he pushed off again, steadily. She could tell he wasn't going to answer her.

For years now, Ba had tried to build the first bicycle factory in China. It seemed an impossible dream, because parts were so hard to obtain. Machined steel. Vulcanized rubber. Chains, springs, spokes. Ba taught her all about it. She knew more about making bicycles than Pang did. So why couldn't she come to Ba's meeting? Ba knew she loved the foundry, and the loading docks, and all the machines and contraptions that he took her to see – she'd much rather be in a factory than a kitchen or a garden.

The grey autumn street offered her no answer. A building under construction swarmed with elbows and knees. The laborers hammered and shouted and threw things to one another. If she closed her eyes, she could almost count the slaps and steps and scrapes of hundreds of hands and feet. And besides the hands and feet, the groans and creaks of wooden axles and clacking poles, like a forest in agony. Only the bicycle passed through the noise with a smooth whir.

They caught up with an armored horse, ambling to the garrison. Astride the tall horse was a metal-clad man, one of the Magistrate's many soldiers. As they passed, Zun glanced up into the soldier's visor and saw an arc of white as the man's eye craned down to look at her. Now she heard a different kind of noise, of weapon against armor, a cold murderous clink. Rough knuckles held a long spear. The metal spearhead was dotted with brown pits. Rust? Or was it the residue of blood?

Ba quickened his pedaling as they passed. Zun peeked past his shoulder at the receding warrior. Ba gave her a don't-worry smile, but the bicycle never lied. Through its steel frame she could feel his legs pull away like a scared rabbit. He covered his flight with a joke.

"That guy rides as stiff as a log. He's got a stomach full of *corrosive vapors.*"

Zun could not help a soft snort. Ba was so silly. Maybe last year, she'd have laughed aloud.

"You know a horse is not bad," Ba said. "I've had a nice horse ride, here and there. But some horses are so moody. Even if you raise them from a little foal, there's no guarantee they won't blame you for sour grain or a sore hoof. Then they bite. The worst are the ones that are *just horses*. 'I am just a horse, I eat straw, kick me I go, pull me I stop.' Ride a horse like that, and your food will have no taste. The sky will not be blue. I can't even look at a horse like that. No. A bicycle – what's a bicycle? A way to move around that makes you happy. Everybody should have one. That's it!"

Zun let go of the bicycle top tube to poke him in the chest. "You're rehearsing," she said.

"And? Was it good? Convincing?"

"Am I your moody horse?"

"If anything, you're my moody bicycle."

"I'd be less moody if you make it so I can come with you tomorrow. Tell Pang no more remarks about – *that subject,* and let me help you with the factory!"

"Hmm, maybe you're a horse."

"Ba!"

"Wang Zun," he said. Her full name – he was serious. "I've indulged you. It's not appropriate for you to go to this meeting. Let it go. You're still a young girl."

Since when do you treat me like a girl? she wanted to say, but dared not. Nevertheless, it was obvious: Ba and Ma didn't raise her to be a typical girl. Zun knew she was fortunate to read and write, and go out with Ba to shops and factories. And she could walk, miles and miles like Ma, because her feet were not bound. But she was alone, a zebra among horses. She didn't even know any girls her age.

She saw them, sometimes: working girls who took care of younger siblings, eyes downcast. Once or twice she caught a black glance, when a flash of temper escaped the veil of duty. Or peeking through the windows of a sedan chair, wealthy girls with bound feet, always with fancy hair combs, slender fingers curled around fans, wide silk sleeves.

She pulled the edge of her own cotton tunic. Zun and Ma had embroidered a row of red pumpkins along the blue cloth. They giggled about it: no one else had a tunic like that. She liked her tunic. But she wanted a seed-pearl hair comb, too.

Ba interrupted her thoughts. "Let's take Ma some cooked food, so she doesn't have to cook." He stopped the bicycle at a street vendor.

Zun was overjoyed. She loved street food, and Ma would be happy when she saw it.

Soon they were home. They lived in an apartment with an adjoining workshop in a compound owned by the Fu family. The building had a traditional gate that led into a square courtyard. Immediately to the left, in the south building, were Ba's workshop and the Fu storerooms. Further on the left, in the west house, was Zun's family apartment, and in the big north and east houses lived the Fu family. A huge willow tree graced the northeast corner. Ba coasted into the courtyard and Zun hopped off. The younger Fu Tai Tai sat by the fountain, peeling radishes while her little son and daughter played in the dirt.

"Jie Jie!" the children cried. "Jie Jie!" They ran to Zun. "Bicycle ride!"

She took them both by the hand to the bicycle.

"Good evening, Fu Tai Tai!" Ba and Zun said.

"Good evening," she replied, her eyes moving only the briefest flutter from her radish. She had lost her youngest baby a month ago. Some things were heavier than a four-hundred-pound coat.

As Ba unloaded the packages of street-vendor food, the Fu children jumped. Zun lifted the five-year-old boy onto the bicycle seat and held him there.

"Two circles, then it's your sister's turn," she said to the boy, and wheeled him around the courtyard. Her stomach growled. She couldn't wait for dinner.

A loud knock at the gate resonated in her chest. *Oh no*, she thought. *Whoever you are, please don't start chatting with Ba. We'll never get to eat.*

A young man popped his head in the courtyard. "Wang Fei!"

"Yes," said Ba. "What is it?"

"The merchants are meeting tonight. Come discuss your factory plans."

"Tonight? I was just about to eat with the family."

"Food is there. Just come."

"All right, all right," said Ba, and the man left.

"Zun-a, tell your mother I can't eat with you tonight. I can't miss this. Take the food in."

"Ba! Why can't you tell her? She's not going to like it."

Ma had ears like a cat. She came out to the courtyard. "What, meeting again? Are they ever going to do anything?" She approached her husband with her arms crossed over her chest and her eyebrows in a tangle. "They're all afraid of the Magistrate. That dried owl turd thinks he can do whatever he wants, including – "

"It's too early to talk of the Magistrate," protested Ba, and Zun did not miss the strange little wiggle of his eyes in her direction. "When we have all the contracts written and sealed, it will be time to take things to the Tribunal."

"Remember those old foxes have been in business much longer than you. They've dug a thousand holes in which to hide. And you have to deal with the government. The shortest path through the Magistrate's office is a wide, wide, circle."

As she spoke, Zun lifted the Fu boy down and picked up his three-year-old sister.

"Step by step," Ba said. "We're making progress."

"Do you have to go *tonight*?" said Ma.

Zun put her face close to the little girl's, and made her giggle. Ma mumbled something. Zun wheeled the bicycle closer.

Ba said, "That's in Shanghai, not here. I'll be careful." He took the bicycle from Zun.

"Well, go on then," said Ma. "Tell those old goats to put brush to paper. Come on, Zun, let's eat."

She smiled goodbye at her husband, until he caught her gaze and smiled back. Ma could never be bothered with silks and hairpins. To her clear oval face and even white teeth, a seed-pearl comb would add nothing.

Ba glided the bicycle to the gate with a grin at Zun.

"And don't say those things about the horses!" Ma shouted. "You never know how some crazy old man feels about his horse."

Zun was still wondering, why did Ma say don't go out *tonight*? What was happening in Shanghai? She ran after Ba to hold the gate open for him.

"Ba, tonight – remember? You said you'd help me with the microscope. You promised."

"You can do it yourself, sweetcake," he said. He pushed off again.

"Ba," she said once more, and he waved and went forward, away from her.

Zun stepped into the street and watched until the rear wheel of the bicycle was swallowed by the approaching night. She closed the gate and walked back to the house. Fu Tai Tai threw out her dirty radish water, and ushered her children inside. It was now deep twilight. All color in the courtyard was gone.

In the kitchen, Ma unpacked the sacks of food that Ba brought. "Cut noodles! Good to eat!" And Zun and Ma sat down to a dinner of dressed cut noodles, boiled tea eggs, and roasted peanuts. Zun said, "Ma, why is Ba meeting his friends at night?"

"In the daytime everyone is busy working. Eat before the flies land on it." Ma bit into an egg. "Anyway, they aren't his friends."

"If they aren't his friends, why is he talking to them?"

"Did you watch the man season these cut noodles? Did he use brown or red vinegar?"

"Brown. Why is he talking to his enemies?"

"Brown. No wonder these are so good. Don't deliberately misunderstand me, Zu-Zu. Your father is building a group of businessmen. They are not all his friends *yet*."

"Why don't you go to the meeting too, Ma? You know more about business than Ba does. He says the numbers make him sleepy and the rules cramp his stomach."

"Because I like to eat my dinner. No more questions!"

Zun ate one peanut, and asked, "Will Ba get in trouble with the Magistrate?"

Ma silently pointed her chopsticks at Zun's bowl and gestured towards her mouth. Zun slowly ate, knowing her mother would not tolerate wasted food.

"You rode on his bicycle all day instead of walking," said Ma. "When I was young, I walked twenty *li* a day to get grass-fuel and water." She set aside food for Ba and covered it. "Don't worry. Your father can talk through anything."

"Ma. What's happening in Shanghai?"

Ma's chest caved in mock exhaustion.

Zun pressed, "Ba used to live in Shanghai, didn't he?"

"Yes, he did."

"So, what's happening there now?" Zun insisted.

"Ee, what doesn't happen there," Ma muttered.

"Ma, really!"

"Ba hasn't lived there for a long time," said Ma. "So they all fan themselves with boredom."

Zun giggled. But she wanted to know more. "But, Ma – "

"*Aiya*, stop worrying!" Ma frowned. "You're getting a big gorge in your forehead."

"Look at your own forehead! It's a freshly plowed furrow!"

Ma leaned in. "Your forehead is a pond – full of flapping geese!"

"Your forehead is a pond – of boiling oil and fish are jumping out of it!"

Ma tried to think of another one, but burst out laughing instead. "Eat. There's nothing to worry about."

Later that night, she dreamed about riding the bicycle with Ba. A young man shot past them, also on a bicycle. More bicycles were approaching them, with old people and young, fat and thin, riding in stately self-absorption. A white dog rode a small black bicycle, its two front paws poised on cupped handlebars. Catching up with the dog, a great dun-colored mare pranced gaily on the four pedals of a bicycle two yards high. In the distance sounded the clash of many gongs. Someone important rounded the corner ahead.

Eight men on silver bicycles pulled a vast wooden bicycle. It was painted red and gold, with carved dragons and demons. High above the street, its plush red seat held an exalted official, holding the tiny ornamental handlebars. This person was swathed in gold-encrusted robes and was wearing a three-horned hat. Zun could not see the face. Was it the Magistrate? The Governor? The Empress herself? The procession came to a stop in front of Zun and Ba, blocking their way. The three-horned hat inclined itself toward her.

"Remove me from this trivial place!" commanded a voice under the hat. A withered hand released the tiny handlebar to point at her.

The eight bicycle riders pushed off in unison.

Zun was so annoyed she wanted to shout. She tried to tell Ba that the official's bicycle was just a stupid cart. But her mouth could form no words. All around her, people rode on bicycles, more bicycles than she had ever seen. She struggled to speak, but they paid no attention to her. She clapped her hands to her mouth and woke up. Her quilt was on the lower half of her face, its rough cotton border on her lips.

Only a dream, only a dream, she thought. But the feeling of being small and voiceless and frightened was so real. She jerked the edge of her quilt tight against her chin and glared at the ceiling. *That's not what my dream was about,* she told herself. *It was not about being quiet and small in front of the Empress it was about bicycles. Everyone's going to have a bicycle.* The thought warmed her, but didn't help her go back to sleep. She couldn't wait to make that thought a reality. She wanted to practice riding the Phoenix herself. She wanted to sew leather over springs for her own bicycle seat. She wanted to look with Ba at the latest shipment of vulcanized rubber from South America. There were so many things to do. If only the morning would come more quickly.

She watched the flickering glow in the doorway. Ma was still up. Why didn't Ma go to bed? Zun couldn't sleep but she was tired, and her thoughts jumbled together. *Ma's not sleeping. Something is going on in Shanghai. Ba sped up to pass the soldier. And the Magistrate: Ba didn't want Ma to talk about the Magistrate.*

She heard a shout outside the house. Was it Ba? Another dream? Out of the night came the clear sound of galloping hooves. Alarmed, she slid out of bed and put on her shoes. She waited, listening.

Ma hissed, "Stay right there!" as she flitted past Zun's doorway.

The gallop abruptly stopped. Zun stood shivering in her thin nightclothes. She heard Ma's quick steps out in the courtyard, and then Ba's voice. A hoarse voice answered back. She couldn't make out what they were saying, but it sounded like the hoarse voice was making commands.

The front gate scraped open. *That must be Ma.*

Ba's voice rang out. "Please don't!"

Ma screamed.

At that terrifying sound, Zun ran outside, across the courtyard. It was a cold night with an opaque black sky and a waning quarter moon. She skidded through the southeast gate.

Just as she entered the street, she saw a man, outlined in hard lines and corners of metal armor, mount a tall horse and gallop away.

Ma was pinned to the wall opposite the street, a hatchet in her right arm. Ba crawled towards her on his stomach, the twisted bicycle behind him.

"Help Ba," said Ma. "Zun-a, help him!"

Zun ran to her father, who had stopped crawling and fell down on his side. There was just enough moonlight for her to see him blinking and struggling to inhale. When Ba saw Zun and felt her hand in his, his eyes crinkled.

She could feel the effort it cost him to smile. A dark stain spread along his side.

"Zun-a," he said, and stopped.

This cannot happen. Her throat constricted, and she tried to cry out, but only a whimper escaped her lips. Her stomach heaved and she doubled over, on her knees beside Ba, still holding his warm hand.

Ma began to moan, a continuous keening sound that pulled Zun to her feet. She ran to the doors of their neighbors and pounded for help, screaming her panic without words.

2. The Taste Of Tears

She could tell without opening her eyes that it was morning. She kept them closed, willing for a few seconds that it hadn't really happened, that last night was not real. She had cried last night, screamed and cried in front of all those people. She hadn't cried like that since she was a baby. And they wouldn't let her be with Ma. So she cried until she was too weak to resist when old Fu Po Po – Grandmother Fu – took her arm and put her to bed.

Now she felt hard and dry as a stone.

"Wang Zun," said a man's voice at her bedroom door. "It's Chiu Yisheng – Doctor Chiu. Please wake up."

Her eyelids scraped over her eyes. Her throat was so dry she began to cough. Chiu Yisheng came to her side with warm tea. Zun gulped the tea.

"I'm very sorry," he began slowly. "Your father's body is with the Fu family – "

Zun put her hands to her face. "How is my mother?"

The doctor swallowed. "She lost her right arm, below the elbow. She needs a lot of rest and time to recover. She is young and strong, but to get well she must take her medicine regularly. She'll have more pain in the next few days. And, she – "

Zun slapped back her quilt and emerged from the bed, fully clothed. A sharp heat had risen in her as she listened to the doctor's deliberate speech. She heard the sympathy and concern in his voice, but she couldn't really take it in. It would mean that everything she saw last night had really, irreversibly happened. She had to see Ma.

"Come," she told him, avoiding his gaze, and marched to the door.

In the kitchen sat a stranger, cleaning her ear with a wire earpick. The doctor scurried forward and gestured to her.

"This is my assistant, Piao Yi. She'll nurse your mother for a week."

The woman smiled. Her teeth were like the overlapping leaves of a big yellow cabbage.

Zun ran to Ma's room and shut the door against the doctor, the woman, and the earpick. The window was draped against the morning light. Ma's right arm, heavily bandaged, lay outside, above her quilt, and her head was barely visible. Zun opened the drapes a little.

Ma didn't seem asleep so much as passed out. Zun pulled the bedclothes back, stared at her face, listened to her breathing, and felt the pulse in her neck. Zun felt her own breathing quicken. She wanted to crawl into bed with Ma, and she wanted to run far away from the strangers in the kitchen. Confused, she closed her eyes. *It can't be true*, she thought. *Please let it be all lies.*

But nothing took away the knowledge that just beyond her eyelids, just past Ma's door, sat those two signposts that said everything had changed. What would that woman do – make soup? Feed Ma? Clothe her? Zun couldn't stand the thought. No stranger would take care of Ma.

She opened her eyes and saw Ba's slippers and hat. Her mouth dropped open to howl, but no sound came out. She couldn't let the doctor and the woman hear. So she sank to her knees and cried and cried. *Don't look; don't look at the hat and the slippers.*

She hid them so that Ma wouldn't see. She scrambled to put away Ba's things: his comb, his bowl of screws and washers, his papers scattered on their dresser.

She heard someone step in the kitchen, and realized that the doctor and the nurse must still be there. The woman would want to be paid! There would be the doctor's bill, and medicine, and rent, and food. They had only a little money saved, and with Ba gone, she couldn't think further. She had to take care of Ma, that was the first thing. She had to march out and take charge.

The doctor and the woman looked at her, not unkindly. Zun felt aware of her puffy face, swollen from crying.

"Tha … ank you for your help," Zun struggled to keep her voice low and even. "I'll take care of my mother myself. My parents both worked outside and I know how to keep the house." She turned to the woman. "I won't be needing your help."

At a nod from the doctor, the woman shrugged and went out the front door.

The doctor stood up as well.

"Doctor, wait." Zun would be officially responsible for everything now. She took a fresh piece of paper from Ma's desk and put it on the dining table. From a cupboard she took a brush, ink stone, and ink. She handed the brush to the doctor.

"Please write," she said.

The doctor looked confused.

"Her medicine, her food, how much she should sleep, when she can walk – write it all."

Zun took back the brush. She wrote on the page, "Medicine." Then she took another page, and titled it, "Food." And another, "Sleep." And a fourth page, "Walking."

"Please, Chiu Yisheng, teach me what to do. Write it all here."

He sat down at the table. Zun watched his every move. He lifted the brush to the first page but it just hung there. Zun got the hint and looked away. The doctor began to write small characters.

"Please write a little larger. I have to be able to read it."

"I'll do my best," said the doctor. He filled the first page with instructions and kept writing.

Zun noticed her hands were cold and she slipped them under her knees. She sneaked a glance at the doctor's brush and saw he was doing a thorough job.

"Thank you, Chiu Yisheng," she made herself say.

For the first few days, Zun was to mix a bitter opium brew for her mother. Ma refused it on the second morning. "I need to be clear. Put it away," she said. An hour later she summoned Zun to talk. Zun could see her breathing was quick and shallow.

"Ma, I think you need the medicine."

Ma gave her head one shake, and smiled at her daughter. "Zun-a, how are you doing?"

Zun surveyed her mother's face. Ma was always sharp and quick, with immediate, restless expressions to match. This morning Ma's face was still, and a thin film of perspiration gave her skin a light sheen. *Ma, your forehead is a plum caught in frost.*

"Come here," said Ma, and Zun buried her face in her mother's left shoulder and sobbed. Ma slipped her left arm around her and reached around with her right. Zun felt the rough cloth of the bandage graze her cheek.

"Don't worry, Zun-a. Ma will get better, and take care of everything."

Zun raised her wet face. "Ma, why? Why did this happen? Who did this?"

Ma shook her head. "I don't know."

"The Magistrate did it! I heard you and Ba talking about him. I know he has those armed men, and everyone's angry about the taxes. It was the Magistrate's man, wasn't it?"

"Zun-a, I doubt it's that simple. You know what I think about the Magistrate – "

"You called him a dried owl turd."

"Yes, but let me say something. Yesterday, your father was in danger, but we didn't know it. Today, we know. We're in danger – and we must protect each other. Do you understand?" Ma's left hand crept out and gripped her daughter.

"I understand, Ma."

"For now, only go to the market and back. Nowhere else. Don't go to your lesson with Kang Laoshi. We don't want to get him in trouble. And Zun," Ma took a deep breath. "Go get the volumes. Bring them all here – and the big clay pot, and a candle."

Zun sat up on full alert. "No, Ma."

"Obey me, Wang Zun."

She walked to the workshop. On several shelves were Ba's books and papers. His books were special, one of a kind – he had copied translations of western mathematicians, Isaac Newton and Leonhard Euler. Ma said papers. Zun collected a small sheaf of loose papers.

"Bring the books too, Zun, the foreign books, science books, bicycle notebooks, all of them."

The books and papers made a few piles as tall as Zun's knees.

"Now then. Take a few at a time, and burn them in the clay pot."

Zun sat still on Ma's bed.

Ma pointed to the first stack of paper with her good hand.

Zun slowly picked up a paper with one hand, the candle in the other. Ma was asking her to do this, and how could she refuse Ma? But this – this was losing Ba all over again. Numb and silent, Zun brought the paper and candle together.

Ma lunged out of the bed and stopped her.

"Wait!" Ma looked like she was going to faint. "Wang Fei, I don't know what else we can do."

Wang Fei. That was Ba's name. Zun blew out the candle at once, and sizzled the wick with spit. "Let me hide them, Ma. I promise I'll be thorough. I'll keep them safe. Please, Ma."

Ma nodded, her arm over her brow. Her face was grey. Zun went to the kitchen and returned with the opium potion, and Ma didn't refuse it this time.

Zun carried the books to the workshop. She found two metal boxes big enough to hold the books. She found wax, and sealed all the cracks in the boxes so they'd be watertight. The writing on the papers blurred as she loaded them in. Ba wrote in dancing, bold characters that only he could draw, but it so hurt to see them – she felt as if each character on the page was a character with a terrible loss, a character that no longer had a living, breathing voice.

She sealed the boxes carefully with more wax.

Where to put them? The canal bank nearby had a shallow slope where she could dig a hole unseen, below the level of the street. But if the water level rose, the tiniest hole in the wax would turn the books to pulp. A hill would be better, but all the hills in the city were covered with walled gardens and houses. Perhaps the courtyard was best. But she'd have to hide all evidence of the hole.

She waited until it was late, and carried the boxes to the courtyard. She picked a spot in the southwest corner, and began to dig with Ma's hoe. The ground was hard, and the hoe crunched against stones. Her heart pounded at every sound, in fear she'd wake someone. *Never mind. Finish this task.* She struck the ground with the hoe in a steady rhythm. Her mind wandered to what Ma had said, about danger. One thing was certain: Ma hadn't told her all she knew. There must be more.

A window in the north Fu house came aglow, and the door scraped open. Clearly the courtyard was a terrible idea! Old Fu Gong Gong –

Grandpa Fu – came out, a candle wobbling in his hand. His long mustache and beard swayed in the night breeze. He was her landlord.

Zun took a step back but he had seen her.

"Wang Xiao Jie – *Miss Wang* – is that you? What are you doing?"

"I'm … gardening, Fu Gong Gong."

"Gardening," he repeated, and sat down on one of Zun's metal boxes. "Ee, what are these boxes? They're cold!"

He looked at the hole Zun had dug.

Zun said nothing. She didn't know what to say to him.

"How's your mother?" he asked. "Did she eat well today?"

"Yes, she did, thank you."

The old man sighed. "Tell your mother it'll be day after tomorrow. Your father's funeral. As she asked."

Zun bowed her thanks and clenched her hoe.

"Well, I better help you. An old man like me doesn't need much sleep." He stood up abruptly and the candle sputtered. He put it down on the box he sat on, and lifted the box up. The books slid inside.

"Books in here," he said, and put the box down and stood with his hands on his back. "Don't put them in the open ground. I have a place under the floor in the south building."

She gaped at him. What an offer that was. So much better than all this digging! But would they be safe? "Fu Gong Gong, my mother doesn't want any trouble – "

"It's no trouble," the old man said. "You didn't tell me what's in there, and I didn't ask. Listen. The noise of your hoe will wake everyone in the neighborhood."

Still she hesitated. Could she trust him? She had scarcely ever exchanged two words with old Fu Gong Gong. He was the respected head of the Fu family; only Ba had dealt with him. But now she had to decide. A risk for her, and a risk for the Fu family too. She knew nothing about Fu Gong Gong, but she knew this. He liked to play elephant chess with Ba on summer evenings in the courtyard, and his laugh rang out whenever either he or Ba made a good move.

He was a good man.

Zun nodded at him.

Fu Gong Gong bent his knees with surprising speed, and picked up the first box of books. She picked up the second. They scrambled to the south building. He opened the storeroom beside the workshop and put the box down. In the dimness Zun made out a wheelbarrow, big clay pots, a loom. Fu Gong Gong pushed the loom aside and showed Zun a place where the ends of several floorboards lined up. He pushed down on one of the boards and it lifted, and another, revealing a dark space beneath. Fu Gong Gong stepped down into it. The floor was at the level of his waist.

"Lift a few more boards, and hand me the boxes," he told her.

When the boxes were in, they replaced the floorboards. Fu Gong Gong pushed the loom back in place.

"Thank you, thank you, Fu Gong Gong," Zun said, bowing low again.

"Go home and sleep," the old man replied. "I'll fill up that dirt hole you made."

She slipped in, washed her hands, and checked on Ma. She was so tired she crawled right into Ma's bed. She wondered what Fu Gong Gong thought about the boxes. He must have had some idea why she was hiding them. But he didn't talk about it – why? *You know why*, she told herself. *Armored horsemen.*

She listened to Ma's quiet breathing and fell into a shallow sleep. In the light of the early morning, Ma stirred.

"I'll help you get up, Ma," said Zun. She peeled back the quilts and supported Ma's shoulder so she could sit up. "Wait." Zun slid slippers on Ma's feet.

Ma put her hand on the headboard and smiled at Zun. "I can stand up myself."

"I'll get your medicine ready."

The kitchen was chilly. She lit a fire of twigs in the small stove and put a few pieces of coal on it. The earthenware pot for boiling medicine had some of yesterday's herbal brew left, enough for this morning. Ma had to drink it warm, with opium drops. She brought a bowlful to Ma, and held it for her to sip. It was hard to hold a bowl of hot liquid with only one hand. When every drop of the medicine was down, Zun helped her lie down again.

"I'll be in the kitchen, Ma."

Zun went there to make more medicine. The doctor had left packages of roots and herbs. It would take several hours to boil the next batch. She sighed. A whole day of chores loomed ahead. Make medicine, shop for food, wash bandages, sweep floors. She took Ma's purse from the little drawer where it was kept and counted their dwindling supply of copper pennies. She didn't know where more pennies would come from – maybe she could take over Ma's letter-writing business. Ba's bicycle factory – she couldn't think about that. It was a dream that had turned into a ghost.

Get the medicine simmering, Zun told herself, *and go to the market.* She put a measure of herbs and roots in the pot, with eight bowls of water, and set it on the stove to heat.

When she came back, she prepared medicine and washed bandages. She boiled rice and vegetables and bones with salt. She helped Ma to the kitchen table.

"Try not to think of it; it won't do any good," said Ma.

"Think of what, Ma?" Zun asked, puzzled.

Ma grabbed at the edge of the table for balance. "Revenge."

Revenge! Zun hadn't thought about it at all. She had a thousand questions still, about the Magistrate, and Ba's meetings, and Ba's books, but she could see that Ma needed all her energy to heal. So she kept quiet and sat down. Dry-eyed, they ate colorless food that tasted like tears.

3. The Official Visit

On the day of Ba's funeral, cold winds snaked under low clouds. Zun held Ma's arm as they watched shovelfuls of dirt fall on Ba's coffin. Ma had paid for a sedan chair to carry her to the cemetery, but insisted on walking the last steps to the grave herself. No one else was there but Fu Gong Gong. Ma hadn't told any of their other friends. "It might not be safe for them to come out in public as your father's friend. Besides, they'll nag me to go to a geomancer, and I refuse. Your father never believed in looking for lucky days." Ma fell silent. Zun knew what Ba liked to say: Every day is a lucky day.

She could not agree with that.

Another long day of chores passed and Zun stumbled to bed. Sleep, logically, should come. But it didn't.

Each night since the armored horseman's attack, when it was quiet, and when she was alone, Ba's passing caught up with her. It made no difference how tired she was; sleep came late, and reluctantly. She'd lie there, trying to rest, and sorrow rose in her like a tide. It was always the same: a wordless, shapeless, limitless ache. She stared up into the black ceiling as her eyes overflowed. She tried not to go to Ma, who she knew slept fitfully in the hold of medicine. So she could only wait until she had cried enough to fall asleep.

The next morning, when Ma was settled beside the warm stove, Zun made herself go to the workshop. The Phoenix was there, still muddy from Ba's last ride. She had not been able to look at it. This was the day she could no longer *not* look at it. Ba had kept it in perfect running order. A sense of duty drove her unwilling feet to the workshop door.

She took the forged spare frame off the workstand and suspended the bicycle on it. She fixed its skewed handlebars with a wrench. She got a clean cloth. When she found specks of dirt, she wiped them off.

Soon the bicycle shone. Its black painted tubes glistened; its nickel-coated handlebars gleamed. The white characters for Phoenix stood out cleanly on the down tube. Even the black rubber pedals refracted small colorful shimmers from the morning sun that streamed through the window.

She had known it would hurt to see the bicycle and be reminded of him, but until she touched it and held it, she didn't know how much she needed it. It was a part of him, and she felt as if she had been drowning and here was a float. She wheeled it around the room and listened to the perfect, even ticking of the bicycle's freewheel. In a strange way it seemed to her like the beat of Ba's heart. Maybe, if she listened every day, her sadness would ease. But it was not to be.

Fu Gong Gong shouted in the courtyard. "They're coming! Open the gate!"

Who was coming? Who could make dignified Fu Gong Gong cry out like that? The courtyard gate scraped open, and Zun scrambled to the window to look. Four uniformed men, the Magistrate's constables, came into the courtyard, followed by two sedan chairs, each held on the shoulders of eight men with cordy necks. A final four constables followed the chairs. The carriers kneeled and lowered the chairs to the ground, side by side. The sixteen carriers, each dressed identically in stiff vermillion jackets trimmed with silver, flanked the chairs in a straight line. The homely Fu courtyard was transformed.

Fu Gong Gong ran before the larger sedan chair, bent to his knees, and put his forehead to the ground. "Welcome to the house of Fu, Honored Magistrate Jiang!" he said loudly.

The sedan chair door slid open. A thin man emerged from the larger chair. The Magistrate! Zun had never seen him so close before. He wore a magnificent silk robe, pale blue embroidered with gold, and a black horned hat. He looked about sixty, with a small curved beak for a nose and bushy grey eyebrows. She could see how he made Ma think of an owl. He nodded to Fu Gong Gong and waved towards the north house. At once, Fu Gong Gong got up and trotted into his house.

The constables ran to erect a small ornate table with a canopy in the middle of the courtyard. The Magistrate placed himself under the canopy, behind the table. Zun gave a little snort. All these people ran around him like whipped dogs – carriers and constables – twenty-four men, and Fu Gong Gong too. She had only a hazy idea why. The Magistrate was supposed to be a gifted scholar who passed the grueling Imperial Examinations. That made him the Empress's local authority. But Zun saw a thin old man in an expensive robe.

The second sedan chair door slid open, and two of the chair carriers ran over to it. Zun held her breath; a woman emerged. She must be the Consort, the Magistrate's young second wife. Even from the workshop window Zun could see her long gown trimmed with pearls, her black hair in fanciful twists, and her tiny satin shoes. Her fingertips barely emerged from her long wide sleeves, and rested like moth wings on the arms of the two big carriers as they guided her out of the chair. She stood behind the canopy and kept her eyelids low.

A constable knocked on the Wang family door.

Ma came out and slowly walked until she was before the Magistrate. She bent down to her knees, her left arm holding her aching right, and painfully lowered her forehead to the ground.

At this, Zun threw her cloth to the floor. She ran out towards Ma.

"Get back to bed! You must rest!" she shouted. As the Magistrate turned to eye her, she remembered to bow.

Ma lifted her forehead and remained on her knees before the Magistrate. "Wang Zun, withdraw immediately!"

Zun was pinned motionless under Ma's fierce glare.

"Your Honor, accept my apologies for my daughter. She does not know her place."

Zun jerked her head down to the level of her knees, and kept it there as she backed away in the direction from which she had come. "My mother requires rest to recover!" she insisted.

The Consort's eyelids remained lowered, but there was a lift of amusement in her shoulders.

Ma did not remark further on her daughter's theatrical exit. Zun closed the workshop door behind her and watched from the workshop window.

The Magistrate began, "In view of the indisposition of the Wang family, a temporary Tribunal is now in session!"

Ma lifted her torso to address the Magistrate. "This humble person is Chen Ru Lin, widow of Wang Fei," she began, in the correct way. "My husband was murdered four days ago. As Father and Mother to our people, I beg Your Honor the Magistrate to find and arrest the murderer, who wanders loose."

Father and Mother to the people: that was the Confucian ideal. *Let's see how much of a father this Magistrate turns out to be*, Zun thought.

"Chen Tai Tai, your request for justice is officially accepted. The Imperial Office is doing all in its power to apprehend the murderer," replied the Magistrate. "We express our official condolences. Wang Fei was a most enlightened man."

Ma bowed again, although Zun could see how difficult it was to do so from a kneeling position.

The Consort nodded at the Magistrate.

"The Consort wishes to present Chen Ru Lin with a gift," said the Magistrate. One of the constables placed a delicate box beside Ma.

"A small token," murmured the Consort.

Ma bowed again. "This humble person is not worthy of the Consort's notice. Most effusive thanks, Lady."

"From one wife to another, I express great sympathy for your sorrows," the Consort said.

Ma's forehead remained on the ground.

"Finally," continued the Magistrate, 'we provide Chen Ru Lin with the accounting of the business levies of Wang Fei." He presented Ma with a scroll. Ma accepted it with her left hand, making no apology.

"We are honored by your visit, Magistrate," she said.

The Magistrate and Consort Lao inclined their heads slightly, and returned to their chairs. The constables removed the temporary bench and canopy. The Magistrate's procession reassembled its formation and left. Ma remained on her knees.

As soon as the gate closed, Zun bolted from the workshop to her mother's side.

"Oh, Ma! Your knees must hurt, let me help you up!"

Ma stood up. She struggled to open the scroll the Magistrate gave her with one hand. Zun reached over and held the scroll open for her mother to read.

Ma's face was grim. "If there's anything you particularly value, hide it," she said. "It seems we owe the Magistrate some fees." The courtyard gate scraped open again. Two of the Magistrate's men stationed themselves there. Ma and Zun looked from the constables to one another.

"Why are they here? We didn't do anything wrong," Zun whispered.

"They aren't here to guard us. They're here to guard the valuables in the house."

"They want to take the Phoenix?"

"Nothing else we have is worth hundreds of taels."

"Oh! He isn't *a* dried owl turd – he's a *thousand* owl turds, with flies on them!"

"Ah, Zun, I shouldn't have said that." Ma checked the constables at the gate. "It's not appropriate."

They stood looking bored. Zun hoped every biting fly in the courtyard would pay them a visit.

"What's in the Consort's box, Ma?"

"Hm?" Ma didn't seem to care. The box from the Consort was covered in fine patterned paper, tied with red silk. "Open it, Zun."

Zun untied the silk cord and slid off the lid. Inside the box was a scroll. At a nod from Ma, she took it out. "Look at the fine handwriting, Ma! Do you think it's the Consort's?"

"Maybe. It looks like a woman's writing."

Zun read aloud:
Alone with my shadow,
I murmur to her,
And write strange words in the air, like Yin Hao.
It is not illness, nor wine,
Nor sadness over the dead,
Like Li Qing Qao, that causes
A nation of anxiety to swell in my heart.
To no one here I can speak
For who can understand me?
My hopes and dreams are more
Than those of men around me,
But our chance of survival diminishes.

What good is the heart of a hero
Beneath my dress?
My life unfolds according to its perilous plan.
I ask Heaven:
Did the heroines of the past
Ever feel this?

A Letter to Lady Tao Qiu, by Qiu Jin

Zun looked up from the scroll in complete puzzlement. Did the subdued Consort have thoughts like this?

"Ma! What does this poem mean?"

"I don't know. It stirs up restless feelings, doesn't it? But not in the best way," said Ma. "I don't care for envy."

"Do you think the Consort is restless? Is she telling us she has the heart of a hero, married to a dried owl – ?"

"Stop! I've really had enough."

"Can I keep this, Ma?"

Ma hesitated. "Yes. But don't read too much into it."

"Oi!" a constable called from the gate. "You there, girl! Bring tea!"

Zun ran for the tea, with the Consort's scroll tucked into her sash.

4. Cookies And Lies

An hour later there was a commotion at the gate. Zun looked out from the workshop window. She was dismantling the Phoenix. She would not allow the Magistrate to set even one dried owl claw on it.

The constables crossed their staffs to block the gate. Someone was trying to get in. Zun heard a commanding female voice, and the constables stood aside with bulging cheeks, chewing.

Two men came through carrying the poles of a sedan chair. The covered chair emerged, and then two men carrying the rear. Behind them shuffled a boy of sixteen in a long silk gown.

"Zhang Ayi!" cried Zun.

The carriers grunted as they let down the heavy chair, and Zhang Ayi tottered out, supported by tiny bound feet and a richly carved cane. She wasn't really Zun's aunt, but Ma's only woman friend among the upper class women of Wanzhou. She was the sister of Ba's friend, the newspaper editor, Zhang Po, and the wife of Canal Engineer Shen.

"Little Wang Zun!" cried Zhang Ayi, and hugged her. "Take me to your mother!" She nodded to the shuffling boy. "Hong, get the food."

Hong was her only child. He fished two heavy wicker baskets from the sedan chair. The exhausted carriers made no move to help.

"I am so sorry about all that's happened," Zhang Ayi said, patting Zun's wrist. "When I heard about the funeral I got up at dawn to boil eggs. First, the flame was too low. Then it was too high. Never right. You wouldn't believe it."

Knowing Zhang Ayi, Zun believed it.

As soon as they were inside, Zhang Ayi shut the door behind Hong and asked, "Why are those constables there? I gave them the cookies I made for you so we could get in."

Zun didn't want to say what was on her mind. Even though the Magistrate's fees were unfair, it would be embarrassing to tell Zhang Ayi that they owed the Magistrate money. "I must help Ma," she said. "We'll be right back."

Ma was already struggling out of bed by herself, and Zun smoothed her hair with a comb. They walked out to the dining room with brave smiles.

Zhang Ayi cried when she saw Ma's bandaged stump. Hong's face became dark red.

"This is unbearable," Zhang Ayi wiped her eyes after a while, 'and you've only eaten half an egg. You must have more, at least four. Well, broth then. Open! Open! Swallow! This one has a goji berry in it; don't forget to chew. Chew more! Think about what you are saying to your stomach! You must *encourage* your organs. Here, try a cake. Remember how Wang Fei loved these cakes?" Zhang Ayi realized her mistake as Ma abruptly stopped eating, and tried to change the subject. "Zun looks like the stem of a cherry."

Ma rallied, and took her cue. "Zun, have some broth at least. You need to keep your strength up. Nothing like Zhang Ayi's broth."

"Nothing like Ayi's broth, Ma," was Zun's return challenge. They faced one another over big bowls of broth, and each glared into the other's eyes until the broth was gone. Zun's stomach sloshed like a boat about to sink, but the broth was warm and tasted of devoted simmering.

Zhang Ayi asked, "What will you do now?"

"We need to settle our debts. That's why the constables are here," said Ma.

"Debts? What debts? I thought you didn't borrow anything."

"The Magistrate added on some fees," said Ma.

"Since when? Did he just make this up?"

"Who knows? But we can't fight his constables."

"This reminds me!" Zhang Ayi counted money from a small silk purse in her sleeve. "My brother sends this. Payment for the last repair."

Ma counted the coins Zhang Ayi placed in her palm. "This is too much!"

"No, it isn't. The printing press needed a lot of work." Zhang Ayi folded Ma's fingers over the coins.

"Tell Zhang Po I'm grateful, but must return half," insisted Ma, holding out the money.

"Tell him yourself," said Zhang Ayi. "He wants to write an article about Wang Fei's case. It will help the Magistrate find the criminals who did it."

Ma dropped her hand to her side and looked very tired. "I don't think that's a good idea."

Zun peeped past the window shade to the courtyard. To her horror, two men, wearing black government office caps, came into the courtyard, followed by two men pushing a cart.

"Ma, some government men are coming!"

The men walked straight to the apartment door, and banged loudly.

Ma took a lingering sip of tea over the noise, then stood up and opened the door to two slight officials. One of them had a long, drooping moustache. He produced a document.

"I am Collector Guo. This is the Seal of Magistrate Jiang," he said, pointing to an official-looking stamp in stylized red characters, "and this is the balance owed. One thousand one hundred and fifty-seven silver taels."

Ma said, "That is no problem. I will pay ten taels now, and discuss the balance with the Magistrate at the next public meeting of the Tribunal. Long live the Magistrate!" Bowing deeply, she placed a small bag of coins in the hand of the other Collector and pushed the door closed. She leaned her back against the door as if to brace it against the Collectors. Zun opened her mouth to speak, but Ma pointed to her mouth and clamped it shut.

Zhang Ayi leaned close to Ma and whispered, "I heard that Collector Guo is a terror! Hide your jewels – "

"I have no jewels."

"Your lacquered bowls – "

The loud banging began again.

"I have no lacquered bowls."

"Your silks ... well, how about furniture? This Collector Guo prides himself on finding the precious things people hide! And he knows all about fine things – vases and valuable scrolls!"

The banging made Ma flinch. "We have none of those things; you know that, he knows that. We were barely making a living, with me writing and Wang Fei fixing machines here and there. We only have the clock and the bicycle, gifts from Lord An."

Zun hissed, "I'm going back to the workshop," and Ma nodded.

As Zun ran from the room, she heard her mother breathe to compose herself before opening the door again.

Zun had to work fast. Ba had collected many tools and devices over the years, but none was as valuable as the Phoenix; none was entirely made of rare machined materials from overseas.

The bicycle lay in pieces on the workshop floor. She decided to put it in Zhang Ayi's sedan chair.

The inner door to the apartment scraped open, and Hong slipped in. He stepped briskly toward Zun. But his steps slowed as he looked around the familiar workshop. He had been one of Wang Fei's regular visitors. "I'm so sorry about your father," he said, and bowed his head so she couldn't see his face. "I'd rather spend one minute with him here than a whole day with my tutor."

Zun didn't want to hear this now. It was a tiny drop of the ocean she felt storming inside her, but the Magistrate's rats were right outside the door.

Hong managed to raise his head and get back to business.

"Our mothers are explaining, arguing, crying, and throwing them bones," he said, "but the Collectors want the bicycle. What are you doing?"

"I've got to get the Phoenix out of here. We'll put it in your mother's chair!"

Hong shook his head. "They're not idiots. Their job is to bring back the bicycle and they won't leave without it. Give it to them. It's not worth your life or your mother's."

Zun knew Hong was right. If the Collectors didn't get the bicycle, Ma would end up in the Magistrate's dungeon for not paying. Her stomach, in a constant knot for days, twisted tighter with defeat. She could not look at Hong. She gazed over her father's shelves: metal tongs, a box of bolts, a sealed jar of white paint. She remembered the poet Kang's shriveled but sure hand brushing the white characters for Phoenix on her father's bicycle, and suddenly felt glad that Hong, the trained classical scholar, was in the workshop with her.

"We'll give them a bicycle!" She ran madly about the workshop. She had two extra wheels, a front fork of heavy cast iron, and a sample frame Ba made from forged tubes. All they had to do was fit it together.

"You can make them another bicycle?" asked Hong in awe.

"Can you paint 'Phoenix' in white on this bar?" she asked, passing him the jar of paint.

She had to figure out a way to join the frame and fork together. There was no time to ride to the foundry and beg Liu One-Eye to braze them. "I'll wire them together. Hong, drop that and hold these two pieces at this angle. Quickly!"

She wrapped wire around the joined ends of the bars. "Hmm. If we could make some paste, and then paint it black," she began, and stopped at the sound of the Wang apartment door opening.

They could hear the Collectors shouting, "Wang Fei kept his work somewhere else. Take us there! Now!"

Inside the workshop, Zun hissed to Hong, "Don't let go! Never mind them!"

They could hear Ma answering the collectors. "This way, over here. Watch out! Don't step there." They could hear a door open – not the workshop door. Zun ran to the window.

"She's taking them on a tour of the Fu building," she said. "Let's hurry now!"

They suspended the frame on the work stand and Hong finished painting the Phoenix characters in white. They bolted in the wheels. On the fork and frame joins, Zun melted the wax she had used to seal the document boxes. It spilled all over the place. She rubbed off the excess and smoothed the join. Then she inked it black. It actually looked very good.

"Hong, bring me that wooden dowel for the handlebar!"

"Wooden dowel – are you sure they won't suspect it's a fake?" he whispered.

"They won't, hardly anyone in this town has ever touched a bicycle," Zun shot back with more certainty than she felt.

Hong looked around the workshop. "What are you going to do with all these tools?"

Zun was puzzling where to put the fake pedal she had made out of wood bound with strips of black cloth. "I don't know. We have to finish this."

Hong brought her more wire. "I can put the real bicycle in the sedan chair, you know, a few pieces at a time."

She looked at him. "Do it. But quickly. They're coming!"

She attached the cranks and pedals to the hub of the front wheel, like an old-fashioned chainless bicycle.

"That looks strange," said Hong. "Pedals on the front?"

"Yes, they move with the front wheel. I don't have another freewheel and chain to put on it."

They heard the Fu apartment door open, and more shouting. "Take us to the bicycle now!"

Zun fanned the new paint on the fake bicycle. "You should go," she said to Hong. "This might not work. You should not risk the Magistrate's dungeon for me."

Instead of answering, Hong grabbed the pieces of the real Phoenix and bundled them through the door, along with as many tools as he could hold.

Ma and Fu Gong Gong were soothing the Collectors. "Of course, of course. How can we keep track of all these things? Just right along here," said Fu Gong Gong, and led them to the workshop door. He gave it a brisk knock just as Hong returned from the apartment.

Hong opened the door. Zun hid her paint-covered hands behind her back. They both bowed to the Collectors.

"Where are Wang Fei's machines?" boomed Collector Guo of the droopy moustache.

"Here is my father's most precious possession," said Zun in a meek voice, stepping back and waving at the bicycle that leaned against the wall.

The Collectors' eyes narrowed and they stepped towards the bicycle, inspecting it. Zun's mouth and throat were so dry she coughed.

"So this is the famous bicycle from Shanghai," said Collector Guo. "Its handle is so ugly and peasantish." He tapped the wooden dowel.

"What are these?" said the other Collector, pointing to the handsome curved pieces of metal above the wheels.

"Fenders," said Zun. "They keep the mud from spattering your robes as you ride." The shiny metal fenders were the only parts she had taken from the real Phoenix.

Collector Guo suddenly stooped to look closely at the middle of the bicycle. "This brushwork is very fine. Emblematic of the Song Dynasty!" he exclaimed, reading the characters for Phoenix on the down tube. The other Collector stooped too.

"Very high-class item! Emblematic of the Song; pays respect to the Tang," he echoed.

Hong's eyes narrowed. He backed away from the bicycle, towards Zun.

"Take it away," said Collector Guo.

Zun stood stony-faced as the Collectors' carriers wheeled the bicycle away. Hong nudged her with his foot, but she didn't move. He elbowed her. She looked at him, annoyed, until he scrunched his face like a little boy who has been kicked.

"*Aiya*, please don't take Ba's bicycle," she wailed. She bent her head and rubbed her eyes. "All his work! All his ideas! Everything went into it! We are lost, lost!"

Collector Guo saw a chance to speak sagely. "Remember the words of Kong Fuzi – Confucius. Hold faithfulness and sincerity as first principles!" The words made Zun bow low and tremble.

In the courtyard, Ma yelled angrily at the sight of the bicycle. "That – " she paused for the tiniest moment when she saw it – "That is worth one thousand taels! How dare you take my child's legacy!"

Zun watched from the workshop window. "There go my spare parts," she said to Hong, feeling a brief surge of triumph. The feeling melted almost instantly as she saw the Collectors' cart piled high with her family's furniture.

"We're not finished," said Hong. "We have to get the real Phoenix out of here."

Zun did not answer. She watched the Collectors mount their horses and follow the cart out of the gate. The Magistrate's guards, with nothing left to watch, took their leave as well.

5. One Step West

In the deepening twilight, Zun followed Hong behind Zhang Ayi's sedan chair.

The Zhang family carriers complained about the weight. "Wa, I thought the Lady was delivering food! Did she bring it all back?"

The dismantled Phoenix, wrapped in cloth together with the tools required for reassembling, was wedged in front of Zhang Ayi's knees.

Ma was clearly tired out, but she linked her left arm in Zun's and urged her to hide the bicycle somewhere safe. "You did well today, Zu-Zu. I don't know if they'll notice they don't have the real Phoenix. Come back soon. We must plan our next step." Zun squeezed Ma's arm and followed the Zhangs out the gate.

When they arrived at the Zhang courtyard, Zhang Ayi got out and Hong took the bundle of Phoenix parts. They waited as the carriers took the sedan chair away to its storeroom.

"Take the bicycle inside!" said Zhang Ayi.

"No," said Zun. "I want to take it away. Less danger for you."

"But what will you do?" asked Zhang Ayi.

"I'll bury it somewhere," said Zun.

"But you can't do that yourself! In this hard ground! I will call the carriers – "

"Better not, Ma, I'll help her," said Hong.

Zhang Ayi stared with shock at her son, who had never done a stroke of manual labor in his life.

"Ma, the fewer the people who know about this the better," said Hong.

"All right then. Wait. I have to do something first," said Zhang Ayi. "Xing! Where are you, Xing?" Zhang Ayi disappeared into the house.

Zun was looking at the ground. "You don't have to," she said. "I can take it away now."

"We should hurry; it's already dark," said Hong. "What's Ma doing?"

Zhang Ayi came back with Xing, who was carrying a hoe, a shovel, twine, and a big oilcloth.

Xing stared at the boy, the girl, and the lumpy bundle.

"Back to the kitchen, Xing, hurry now." Zhang Ayi gave Hong and Zun workman's jackets and hats. "People will wonder what a girl and a scholar are doing with peasant tools in the night," she said. "Wrap the Phoenix in oilcloth – protect it – and then use this cloth for a sack."

"Thank you, Zhang Ayi!" Zun took the twine, uncovered the Phoenix, and carefully tied its components together. She attached the wrenches for the wheels and handlebars to the top tube – the horizontal tube between the seat and the handlebars. She replaced the cloth cover and wrapped the oilcloth around the whole bundle as tightly as she could. She bound it with several loops of twine.

Zhang Ayi addressed Hong, who held the hoe and shovel openmouthed. "Work quickly, and don't bury it too deep, and not too shallow, and not near a tree, at least twenty-five paces from water, and be quiet, but make some noise to scare away snakes; avoid all areas with frogs because, *aiya*, they will croak and croak and croak, and if – "

"Ma, frogs croak in the spring," said Hong, pushing her aside.

"Zhang Ayi, good bye!" Zun hoisted up the Phoenix, holding the cloth end over her shoulder, and stumbled away with it.

"Let me carry it," called Hong, shuffling after her with the tools.

But Zun hastened to the Zhang family gate. Once outside the gate, she said, "Hong, lend me the tools. You stay home."

"You can't do this yourself!"

"What I can't do is return your favor. This is too much!"

Hong did not know how to answer, so he began walking with the tools. Zun followed. She struggled to find words to make him go home.

"I'll just go myself, I don't need the tools." And she headed in the opposite direction. Hong caught up and stayed behind her. Zun tossed her thoughts over her shoulder.

"You'll get extremely dirty."

"I can wash."

"You'll break your fingernails." Hong bore the long fingernails of a traditional scholar.

"They'll grow back."

"Your tutor will shun you when he smells the traces of manual labor."

"I shun my tutor. Especially his fingernails."

"What would your father think of this?"

"*Your* father would think that this bicycle should be saved by anyone who values it!"

"You don't even know what that means!"

"I've heard you talk about it often enough – you and your father."

This silenced Zun.

"Where are we going?" he asked, and she quickened her pace in reply.

She headed west, to the edge of the city. The oilcloth-wrapped Phoenix was very heavy and awkward to carry. The hard edges dug into her. Sweat coated her neck and forehead and stung her eyes. Occasional puddles of light from restaurants and shops were not enough to reveal all the potholes and bumps in the road, and every now and then she stumbled.

"My turn," said Hong.

"Twenty steps more," Zun grunted.

Outside the city wall there was an empty stretch of fields, beyond a roadside shrine. The shrine would help her remember where the bicycle was buried. They simply had to pass through the West Gate, which was manned by Imperial sentries.

Hong was carrying the Phoenix when they saw the torches of the West Gate.

"We're going to the open land beyond the gate? How will we get by the guards? Do you have a plan?" asked Hong. "Still no answers, eh?"

"How can I think when you keep asking obvious questions?" asked Zun, who was not at all sure how to get through the gate.

"Well, stop then, I need to breathe," said Hong.

"Must you? I don't want to leave my Ma alone too long," said Zun.

"Just wait. I have an idea." And Hong put down the oilcloth bundle, and wiped his forehead and neck with his sleeve. Zun waited. But Hong did nothing.

"Well? What is the plan?"

"Wait."

"Wait? Maybe you should go home."

"No, just wait. I'm telling you, wait."

They waited, and Zun was about to drag the Phoenix from Hong and continue on her own, when a farmer led his oxcart from a side street onto the main road. Hong ran to him. "Sir, we need a ride to the west."

"Sir, is it?" said the farmer. "No one ever called me 'sir' without – "

"Ten copper pennies," Hong blurted. "For me and my friend, to ride in your cart."

"Twenty."

"Twelve."

"Twenty."

"Fifteen – that's all I have!"

"Twenty."

Hong walked away. The farmer called out, "Fifteen, then."

Hong fished out exactly fifteen copper coins, being careful not to jingle any remaining coins. Hong and Zun clambered onto the cart, setting the Phoenix between them, and tried to look like the bored sons of the farmer, heading home. Under the gatehouse torches, two Imperial guards scrutinized all who came through. They passed through the gate without incident.

When they hopped off the farmer's cart, Zun held Hong's sleeve. They waited several minutes after the creak of the farmer's wheels died away. Zun led them to the shrine. Behind it, away from the road, rose a small hill. As Hong followed, he became nervous.

"You're going to put it in a cemetery?"

"No, next to one. There are trees on the edge."

They scrambled up the hill and Zun picked a spot. They put down the Phoenix. Hong took the shovel and Zun started with the hoe. They both hacked at the cold ground. The moon hid behind clouds. It was very difficult to make progress. When she hit a rock, she had to dig around it until she could get the hoe under it. Hong pulled and struggled with tufts of roots. He didn't complain, but rubbed his blistering hands on his robe. Zun tore four strips from the outer cloth around the Phoenix, and they wound it around their hands.

After what seemed like hours, Hong let loose a whoosh of breath and threw himself on the ground. "Are you sure you want to do this? I think we should hide it at my house," he pleaded.

Zun paused. She was flagging too. The hard handle of the hoe burned into her hand. She glanced at the long form of the boy stretched out in the darkness. For some reason, she couldn't stand the thought of the Phoenix trapped in Zhang Ayi's house. If only she could assemble the bicycle right there and ride off, away from the Magistrate. But Ma couldn't come with her. Ma had to get better, and then they would dig up the Phoenix together. *This is only temporary.*

"Go on home if you're tired," she said. "I'll finish here." She gripped the hoe and hacked it into the pit. The cold ground crunched and pushed her back. She hacked and hacked some more. She could no longer feel her hands, but it didn't matter. Hong sat upright in his spot and stared. She saw him slink up and join her. But the call and answer of the dirt and the hoe were all she cared about now.

The grey glow of dawn crept from the east as they finished. They headed back to the city, toward that weak winter light.

The early morning time was an advantage. They re-entered the West Gate with farmers bringing vegetables to market. Zun's mood lifted. They'd succeeded; they'd kept the Phoenix safe.

"Thank you, Hong. Please take your jacket and the tools," she said.

"Keep going. I'll walk you home," he insisted.

When they got to her gate, she tried again to return the workman's jacket she borrowed, but he made a big show of waving fumes from his nose. "Keep it," he said. "You'll never wash it clean." They both chuckled.

"Your mother's waiting. You better hurry," she said. Hong limped towards his home.

Zun closed the gate behind her. Despite her exhaustion, her heart lightened more than it had in days. The dawn was all hers. She tiptoed across the dim, silent courtyard and imagined the Fu family and her mother asleep and unaware of her secret night of digging.

She was wrong. Zun's apartment door hung open like a bird's broken wing, and inside, the apartment was empty. Ma was gone.

6. Yin Ayi

Panic rose in Zun's chest. She checked the workshop. No Ma. She returned to the kitchen and paced. Someone grabbed her shoulder from behind. Zun gasped in terror and wheeled to face Fu Tai Tai, who looked furious. Fu Tai Tai dragged her across the courtyard to the east house, her own house, and closed the door.

"Where were you – I've been waiting for you! The Magistrate's men took your mother to prison," whispered Fu Tai Tai. "She said you must leave! They'll come back for you!" She gave Zun a cloth sack with some food and a bowl for water, and pressed money into her hand.

"Listen, Wang Zun. Your mother was afraid this might happen, and she made a plan. You must go to her home village, where she grew up. Go out the West Gate. At the village, find a woman named Yin. Ask Yin Ayi for the Old Squirrel. You understand? Old Squirrel. Yin Ayi will know." Fu Tai Tai looked at Zun's head. "Always wear this hat and pretend you're a boy."

"What about Ma? What did they do with her? Are they going to kill her?"

"No." Fu Tai Tai was firm. "No, the Magistrate is afraid of rebels. He'll keep her alive and try to get information from her."

Zun didn't like the sound of that at all. "Ma's not a rebel!"

Fu Tai Tai shook her head and shrugged her shoulders. She threw up her hands. "No, of course she isn't! These are crazy times." Her voice trailed, and she looked at the door to her left, where Zun knew her children slept. She sighed and gently pushed Zun toward the front door. "Go now, and hurry!"

As she opened her door, Fu Gong Gong opened his door too and ran across the courtyard.

"Take her out the side door, not the main gate," he said. He and Fu Tai Tai led her to a door at the back of the east house.

Zun bowed low to the Fus. "Thank you for everything. My parents' things are in the apartment – will you keep them for me?"

"Of course," said Fu Tai Tai.

"Did your father teach you elephant chess?" Fu Gong Gong asked. Zun nodded.

"They captured your mother, but the game's not over yet. Keep playing. Play to win."

She bowed again, and walked through the door into the small alley behind the east house. It was still dim; the sun hadn't reached it yet. Soon she found herself again on the road to the West Gate.

In a few blocks, she turned north. Even with Fu Tai Tai's urgent voice ringing in her ears, she had to see where they took Ma. Ma still needed medicine. What if her fever returned?

The city woke. She could smell lit fires, and hear doors scrape open. She passed some of the carts she had seen earlier when she reentered the city with Hong. The government buildings loomed ahead. In front were the massive doors of the Tribunal building, where the Magistrate held office. Stone carvings flanked each door, and a huge sign proclaimed the authority of the Imperial Government. The doors were shut and silent.

Zun walked around the high stone walls that surrounded the Magistrate's compound. Inside were the Magistrate's house, the prison, and the new garrison. Armed men stood at every portal. There was no sign of Ma.

When she returned to the front of the Tribunal, a man scurried out towards the noticeboard. He pasted a fresh paper notice. When he left, Zun read it. It was still early; she was alone. The notice read:

Anyone with information about the recently deceased rebel Wang Fei, please report immediately to the Magistrate.

Rebel! Now they call Ba a rebel!

Wang Zun, the daughter of Wang Fei and Chen Ru Lin, is at large. There is a reward of five taels for information on her whereabouts, and twenty taels for her delivery to the Tribunal.

Fu Tai Tai was right! They wanted her too! At the bottom of the notice was a crude line drawing of a girl, which could have been anyone. Thankfully, they seemed to know no details of her appearance.

Zun looked around. No one paid any attention to her. Some men strolled up to the noticeboard and she casually ambled away, glad for her hat and the bulky workman's jacket.

She slipped into an alley and squatted against a wall, sank her head on her knees, and thought.

Maybe she should just let them take her. Then she'd be with Ma. She could spend the money Fu Tai Tai gave her on some medicine, then go in. She could make sure Ma took it.

But if she did that, how could she help Ma get out? And she would be disobeying Ma.

Maybe she should get coal and sulfur and nitrates and make gunpowder – Ba had shown her how. Enough gunpowder would make the Magistrate's walls come down. But she'd have to stay hidden in the city to make her explosives, and she didn't have enough money to buy all the materials she needed.

The red embroidered pumpkins on the hem of her tunic peeked from under her jacket. A giveaway! With trembling fingers, she pulled at the edge of her tunic. She thought of Ba's sharp shears, Ma's sewing scissors. Did the Collectors take them? She had been so focused on saving the Phoenix, she didn't know. She picked out the pumpkins, thread by thread. The hem of her tunic now looked horrible, ragged and dirty. She rolled the red threads into a ball and pressed it into the mud. Now the red was black. She might as well go through with Ma's plan. She'd go to Yin Ayi for help.

It was a day-and-a-half's walk from the West Gate to Chen village. She passed through the gate without incident, walking with a group of farmers as if she were one of them.

Ma had left Chen village but never gone back. Her parents had not forgiven her for marrying Ba instead of the farmer they had chosen for her. Ma had never brought Zun there. But Ba had.

He had ridden her there one morning on the Phoenix. He stood in a field and pointed out the little cluster of buildings where Ma had grown up. He showed her the pond where he had first seen her catching frogs with the children. "I kept sneaking back to Chen village to see her. One day I walked up to her and scratched a poem in wen yan, classical Chinese, with a stick in the mud around the pond. I was just about to read it to her when *she* read it to me! Then she said, "Not bad. But the carp in this pond never grow that big." And you know what happened next – "

"The matchmaker," Zun said.

"If I had to choose between a hungry tiger and that Chen matchmaker, I'd pick the tiger. Her piercing screams, her bulging eyes! The manure balls she threw at me! But I'm so grateful to her, because I asked, "Chen Tai Tai, how does this young lady know how to read?" and she yelled, "Chen Ru Lin! Get inside immediately!" And that was all I needed to know. Chen Ru Lin – your mother's name. I wrote to your mother that same day."

Zun shook her head. That was how her parents had met. The strange thing was, Zun knew that Ma missed the village. Even though she'd left the countryside behind, Ma was no city woman. She hoed her vegetables in the courtyard and disposed of any vermin that plagued the Fu family. It would be interesting to be in the place where Ma grew up. Zun quickened her steps.

At midday she spent a few copper coins on some bread and a tea egg. When it grew dark, she was many *li* from a food stand, in open countryside. She was exhausted, with no sleep the previous night when she buried the bicycle. The cold wind that had started at sunset blew stronger. She stumbled into a field and surrounded herself as best she could with straw and dead weeds. Her feet and legs ached from her long walk and she was glad to stop moving.

In the stillness, her sorrow caught up with her. The empty black sky was vast and she was alone. She sat up to blow her nose and heard the wind blow over dead winter grass. Her nose cleared, she caught a whiff of the night smell, of damp earth and mixed weeds. She was far away from the acrid smoke smell of the city. She made a pillow of coarse pokey stalks and curled up on her side.

She woke up shivering. It was still night, and miserably cold. She got up to walk.

For a few hours, her mind was completely blank. It was cold and dark, she had to keep moving, and the ground was bumpy. She became thirsty, but couldn't see any streams. This was only her second day away from home, but already she felt she was in a different world.

As the sun came up she crossed a small irrigation ditch. She was so thirsty she dipped her bowl into it and drank. She let herself rest and dozed on the bank. When she woke, a diffused white light flooded the overcast mid-morning. She trudged on, and a couple of hours later reached Chen village.

She wasn't sure how to approach it. In the surrounding fields men and women dug roots for the late harvest. She decided to march straight into the cluster of houses that made up the village. Small children trickled out of their courtyards and followed her. Grubby-cheeked country children, bundled in winter coats – *my cousins*, she thought.

A man sat on a wooden stool fixing a hoe. His hands looked huge, but Zun saw they were all knuckles and bones. His cheekbones stood out sharp below glittering black eyes. He stared at Zun but did not say a word.

She stopped before him and bowed.

"Please, sir, I am looking for a woman named Yin," she began.

"City kid," said the man. "What's a Wanzhou kid doing here alone?" He looked around her and past her, for other people.

"I am Wang F … Feng," Zun stammered. She should have worked out more carefully what she had to say. She didn't know it would be so obvious where she came from.

"What do you want with Yin?" asked the man.

"My mother has a message for her," said Zun.

The man narrowed his eyes. "Who's your mother?"

"My mother is Yin's niece. We have news about her cousin's wedding. Please, where does Yin Ayi live?" Zun was not used to this.

"Yin is too busy to go to any wedding," said the man. "And Yin never said anything about cousins in the city."

"Oh yes, we moved to the city many years ago. Please let me deliver the message to Yin Ayi," Zun insisted.

"Or what, city kid?" he said softly, in a way that made Zun's stomach drop.

She didn't know what to do. The children crowded around her. A few of the boys, she could see, had rocks in their hands. If Ma still lived here, she'd have read stories to them. Zun decided to tell the village man the truth.

"I'm not a stranger. My mother grew up here. Her name is Chen Ru Lin and she likes fried chicken!"

"Chen Ru Lin? The one who reads and writes?"

Zun nodded.

The man stared into Zun's face. "Well, she kept you fed, at least," he said. "I'll let Yin deal with you. Follow me."

Zun and the children followed him to the smallest house in the village, more a hovel than a house. Its one window was shuttered with crude boards. He knocked at the door.

"Open it!" called a voice. Zun couldn't tell if it was a man or woman. At the sound of the voice, the children scattered. That seemed like a bad sign.

The man opened the door to a featureless dark. "Go in," he said.

This is what you asked for, thought Zun, taking small steps into the dark hovel. The man closed the door behind her.

A dim figure stepped under the patch of grey light that filtered from a chimney vent in the ceiling. Zun made out a round bald head and bulging blue-blob eyes. She gasped in fright.

"I'm Yin," the figure said. "You're only a child!"

Zun heard rummaging. Yin lit a match, and the flare of light showed her soft cheeks and a little smile. She lit a candle.

"Don't be frightened. I don't need light, but you do. Sit over there," she waved the candle towards a table and stools. "Who are you?"

Zun wondered exactly what to say. She sat on one of the stools and took a good look at Yin who sat before her. The wrinkles on her neck meant she wasn't young. She obviously couldn't see anything through those clouded eyes. How did she know Zun was not an adult? Yin sat up straight and seemed very confident for an old blind woman. She wore pale orange robes – nun's robes.

"Yin Ni Gu," Zun began, "I am Wang Zun, daughter of Wang Fei and Chen Ru Lin," she said quickly.

"Chen Ru Lin's girl! Oh!" cried the old woman, and lifted her hand quickly to Zun's face. Zun flinched. Yin withdrew her hand, and the little smile returned to her face.

"You didn't know, did you? I taught your mother to read and write," said Yin. "Call me Yin Ayi."

Zun remembered now, that Ma had said she learned from a nun who had returned to the village to take care of sonless parents.

"I've missed Chen Ru Lin all these years! How is she?" Yin Ayi asked.

"She's in prison. The Magistrate thinks she's a rebel," Zun stammered. "But that's not all." It was surprisingly hard to say the rest. Zun maintained a monotone. "Wang Fei, my father, is dead. And my mother lost her right hand."

Yin Ayi's hand lifted towards Zun again, more slowly this time. "Please," she said. "Let me see you." And her fingertips traced Zun's face. "You look a lot like your mother."

Many things sprang into Zun's mind. *What was Ma like? Do I have many cousins here? Did you know Ba too?* Instead, her stomach gurgled loudly.

Yin Ayi sprang up. "Don't move – I'll cook you something!"

Zun remembered her errand. "Yin Ayi, my mother said to go to the Old Squirrel."

"Uh. *Him?*" Yin Ayi snorted and lit a fire in the stove.

"May I help you cook, Yin Ayi?" asked Zun.

"You rest, Wang Zun." She put a pot of liquid on the fire. A brothy smell warmed the room.

"The Old Squirrel is a man?"

"I believe so," said Yin Ayi. She stirred the broth and threw in chopped turnips. "I'm sorry I have no grain. The Magistrate just collected the harvest. We're living on roots until the winter wheat comes in."

"The whole village?"

"Yes, the whole village," Yin Ayi replied.

That explained the man's sharp cheekbones, and the children's big eyes.

Yin Ayi shook her head. "Anyway, this Old Squirrel, he lives far up in the hills, with his two boys. He's a wu shu – martial arts – teacher, an old friend of your parents. Call him Shifu – Master. He's quite vain about his skills, although what good they've done him I don't know. Do you know, when those two boys were babies, he used them for kung fu practice! He'd rock them to sleep, and then balance them on his knees or elbows, trying to keep them asleep. If they woke up, he'd begin again."

"Maybe I should go back to the city," said Zun doubtfully. "I must find a way to rescue my mother."

"If your mother wants you to find him, I'm sure she has good reasons," said Yin Ayi. "And if an old man spends years learning to act like a squirrel – what's a mere nun to say about it?" She put a steaming bowl of soup on the table. "Now eat!"

Yin Ayi's rich vegetable soup gave Zun a brand new stomach that was warm and full and happy.

"Spend the night here," insisted Yin Ayi. "You must be tired."

"I must go as fast as I can," said Zun. "My mother's not well – she hasn't recovered from her wound."

"Hmm." Yin Ayi grunted in agreement. "Avoid anyone on the roads. Many bandits prowl around – that useless Magistrate! Keep your money well hidden. And tell no one where you're going. Say you're going to Bamboo Hill." She gave Zun detailed directions to Shifu's hideout and made her repeat them.

"Goodbye, and thank you," Zun whispered.

"I'm sorry about your father and mother," murmured Yin Ayi.

Zun nodded, and walked off. She wished Yin Ayi had not said that. She began her long, cold walk as her eyes blurred with tears.

7. Forest March

After midday she came to a village, bigger than the tiny Chen. The center of the village was a crossroads, and the area around the crossroads was a marketplace. She saw a barber, shaving the top of a man's head, a meat vendor's stall, with hanging strips of pork and sausage, and people selling vegetables and pickles. One stand sold warm food.

"How much for a bowl of noodles?" Zun asked, sitting on a stool.

"Five copper pennies," said the proprietor.

"Five?" Zun couldn't believe it.

"It's after harvest. You can't get noodles for less."

"That makes no sense. After the harvest there's plenty of grain," Zun spoke without thinking.

The woman shrugged. The warm steam from her soup pot smelled so good. Zun imagined fresh chewy noodles and couldn't resist. She put five copper pennies on the table. The woman snatched them up.

As they waited for the noodles to cook, the woman tried to chat.

"Quiet little boy – a scholar, eh? Clouds in the northeast tonight; I wouldn't head that way." Zun did not respond. She watched a goat.

The woman gave Zun a bowl of noodles, and tried again.

"Nice tunic you have – such quiet colors, and thread so fine. I heard you could buy cloth like that in Wanzhou."

Zun shot the woman an alarmed look.

"Maybe you'd like to trade that tunic, that nice Wanzhou tunic?" smiled the noodle woman.

Think! I am a boy on an errand. She belched as loud as she could. "Hot sauce, please!" she bellowed. She pretended to catch a body louse from her neck and squeeze it dead.

"I don't have hot sauce," said the woman.

Zun shoveled the rest of the noodles down her throat, being careful to slosh soup on her tunic and wipe her mouth on her sleeve.

She walked briskly out of the marketplace and onto the south road. As soon as she was out of sight of the market, she turned west. Past the fields encircling the village, she struck out on another road that led into a patch of dark woods.

As she entered the woods, Zun felt uneasy. Thick branches could conceal followers. She thought she saw a moving shadow ahead, to the left. She quickened her pace. Did that nosy noodle woman tip off bandits? *I made a huge mistake – I overpaid for those noodles, and now she thinks I'm rich.* Zun gripped the strap of her cloth bag. Just that morning, Yin Ayi had warned her to avoid people on the road. But the road seemed safer than the shadowy trees.

Zun picked up an arm-sized tree branch and resumed walking. In the distance ahead, two grey figures stepped onto the road. Zun hesitated. Where could she go? The two figures walked towards her.

She felt a vibration, accompanied by a growing rumble on the road behind her. The two figures melted into the trees. Zun picked out the sound of hoofs. She started for the edge of the road, but a soldier on horseback rode right up to her. He led a small mounted force of ten men, followed by about thirty foot soldiers. They wore the insignia of the provincial Governor, the official one step higher than the Magistrate. Zun stood up straight.

"Honored Commander!" she cried.

The mounted leader halted the troop. "What is it, boy, you have something for us?"

Zun bowed low. "Honored Commander, there are bandits on this road. I am going home to my village. Please, let me run with your troops!"

"Who are you and where are you going?"

"My name is Wang Feng. I'm going to my native village on Bamboo Hill. My father – "

"Go to the middle of the infantry. Men, make way!"

The company resumed its march. Zun felt a lot safer. It was hard to keep up with the long legs of the men, but it was better than carrying a tree branch and fearing every shadow. She glanced at the men around her. To her right was a thickset man with a sword. He had a rocking gait and looked straight ahead, but never at her. On her left was a younger soldier. He seemed livelier; he checked the woods alongside, and glanced at Zun and gave her a little grin.

After a while, Zun faltered. She was tired. The young soldier on her left reached for her bag, and Zun snatched it away.

He smiled at her. "Wang Feng, let me carry it for you," he said.

Zun thought about it, and shook her head.

"Going to Bamboo Hill, are you?"

Zun nodded at him.

"Going home to your parents?"

Zun nodded again.

"In a few months I'll see my son," said the soldier. "He's about your age. You're not far from Bamboo Hill now – you'll see *your* parents tonight."

Zun tried not to cry at that. The soldier glanced at her and got alarmed.

"Don't you want to go home, boy?"

"Oh yes! I can't wait! I can't wait to see my parents," said Zun, struggling to grin.

An hour passed. It grew dark, and the troop reached a crossroads.

The Commander halted everyone and called back. "Wang Feng, here is your path!"

The young soldier led her to the front of the company.

"This is the way to Bamboo Hill. We go the other way," said the troop leader.

Zun bowed. "Thank you, Honored Commander, for the escort."

"There is the fee," he said.

"Fee? You did not mention any fee."

"Imperial protection along this road costs ten taels," said the Commander.

Zun took a step back. "I don't have ten taels!"

"What do you have, then?"

"My family paid taxes already!"

"But you did not pay for this service, did you? The protection of an entire armed unit?"

"I didn't ask – "

"But you did ask."

Zun reached into a pocket. "I can give you one tael," she said, fishing out a silver coin.

The Commander rolled his eyes. "Look in his pockets," he said to the young soldier.

The young man hesitated.

"Check him for money, and take it. Let's go; I don't want to miss dinner." The Commander leaned forward in his saddle and glared. "There's time tonight for a flogging."

Red-faced, the young soldier put his hands in Zun's sleeves to feel for more money. He pulled out the Consort's scroll that Zun still kept in her sash.

"Give me that," said the Commander. He unrolled it and scanned it. He looked sharply at Zun. "What's this?"

"It's ... it's a poem, Honored Commander," said Zun.

The Commander looked at the scroll again. "What's it about?"

He couldn't read it! Zun was surprised.

"It's a letter to a lady."

"What're you doing with wen yan – classical writing?"

Zun squirmed. "My cousin wrote it."

"Check him all over; he's got more money." The Commander threw the scroll over his shoulder.

The young soldier ran his hands over her body to check for hidden pockets, and when he passed over her chest, she whipped his hands back for a second. Now Zun's ears burned. He tinkled some coins in her trouser pocket and drew them out.

The Commander counted the money in his palm.

"Ee, five and change. Hardly worth bothering."

Zun stalked away from them down the road to Bamboo Hill. She didn't get her scroll back. The young soldier caught up with her. She did not slow down or look at him. He stuffed Zun's pocket with bread, and ran back to his company.

As soon as the army was out of sight, Zun left the road and picked her way through the underbrush.

She found a patch of ground enclosed with bushes, open to the sky. She spread a cloth from her sack on the ground and curled up close to the drooping branches. What a relief to be alone! She listened to the soft sounds of breeze and forest, while stray flecks of starlight burned in her unsleeping eyes.

8. The Old Master

The smell of scrambled eggs fried with green onions was crueler than a slap in the face. Zun squatted in a cold bean barn hunched over a bowl of thin rice gruel. All afternoon she had gathered vines in a bean field, her labor in exchange for a night's shelter. When the sun had set, Zun followed the farmer back to the house. She could smell the rice that was nearly done, and the eggs frying.

The farmer had said, "How about you stay a few more days, finish the bean harvest?"

"I'm afraid that I can't – I must travel on in the morning," Zun stammered.

"Mm. You sleep over there." The farmer waved at the bean barn. "I'll bring your meal." And he brought her the bowl of gruel and a grubby little candle.

Not even a pickle in it, she thought. *At least it's warm.* She slurped up every drop and lay down on a pile of bean vines. Something crawled out from under her – probably a spider. The vines crackled at her slightest movement, but they were more comfortable than the ground. She managed a grim smile. It was almost funny. That farmer probably thought he was teaching her a hard lesson for not helping him with the harvest. After the lessons she'd had lately, a skimpy meal was nothing.

She blew out the candle, and the familiar sorrow weighed on her. She lay there, waiting for its grip to loosen. Hours passed before she finally slept.

She woke with a start early the next morning, and bumped her head on the empty gruel bowl. She didn't feel like asking the farmer for breakfast. She had saved the last bit of the soldier's bread in her pocket; she'd eat that on the road.

The road went uphill, steeper and steeper, past terraced fields. The path dipped down and died in an unexpected little gully of dense bush. Yin Ayi's directions had been clear up to this point: to get to the highest point of the hill above the terraces, but she must have taken an offshoot of the main path. She had to backtrack again. First she needed a rest. She sat against a boulder and flopped her legs out in front of her. Looking up, she saw a tree in late autumn color, its leaves a net of translucent yellow tongues against the sky. *I wish Ba could see this*, she thought. And her lonely grief cascaded on her.

She had never before understood what death brings. It was not the end of Wang Fei's life that she mourned; it was the loss of so many beginnings. It was the loss of all beginnings. She'd taken it for granted that they would do so many things: see Shanghai, build her own bicycle, eat her aunt's famous sausages, travel to the hills of Guilin, even go to the foundry and cast a pedal. No time, no place felt real without Ba there beside her. Now she was left in this horrible, passing, false world where she had nothing, and everything changed in the course of a day. Today, a walk down terraces. Tomorrow, what? She had no idea. What did it matter, for Ba lay in the cold ground. She dropped her face to her knees and cried in misery, until she was so exhausted she dozed off.

When she awoke it was already dusk. She retraced her steps to the main path, and followed the sharp curve of the switchback.

She came to a small clearing. A rough fence enclosed a vegetable garden in front of a weathered grey shack. A paper-shuttered window leaked pale light. Smoke rose from a clumsy little chimney. It looked just as Yin Ayi had described it. Zun hobbled to the door as fast as she could, and knocked.

An old man opened the door. He wore a glowing clean pale grey jacket, sash and matching trousers. His head was a perky freckled egg, framed by wisps of mottled grey hair. At the sight of Zun, his eyebrows rose in suspension above relaxed and sleepy eyelids.

"Shifu," Zun began, bowing.

"Wang Zun," he said, and bowed back.

How did the old man know her name? Zun could only nod.

"Come inside and rest!" he urged.

Zun followed the old forest man inside, but kept her eyes wide open. The room was square and neat, with one doorway into another room. In the far left corner was a small narrow bed. To the right was a fireplace, with a pot on a stand. A delicious rooty smell issued from the pot. Some low cupboards made for storage space and served as a kitchen counter in the corner opposite the bed. Two boys, about her age, turned and leaned towards her to stare – homely, country boys, one thin and one thick. They were the first boys she had seen who did not wear the required Manchu hairstyle, with the front of the head shaved and a long braided queue in the back. The thick one had long bangs of hair that he swept to the side. The thin one's head was covered with short tufts. A crude table and three stools stood in the warm place in front of the fire. Under the table rested a black and white pig.

Shifu swept a hand towards the boys. "Wang Zun, these are my students, Hing Li and Hing Han."

Zun bowed, and checked to see how low the boys were bowing. They all corrected to the same level.

Shifu goaded his household into action. "Li, get Pig-Pig out of here. Get more wood and water. Han, get the soap. And the needle box." The thick boy and the pig trotted past Zun out the door, and the thin, tufted boy turned to the cupboards. She stared at the pig's drooping eyes and solid round cheeks, and noticed Shifu staring at her.

"Shifu, I'm here because – "

"No talking! I know, I know all about Wang Fei." He shook his head and blinked hard. "Now, you've had a long journey," he said, "Come here first – you must wash. Dirt is an insidious enemy." He took her to the counter and poured a basin of water. He waited while she washed her hands and face with soap beans.

"Give me your hand," he said.

Zun complied, and he felt her pulse, looking blankly ahead. Zun knew what he was doing; she had been to the doctor before. She drew her hand away.

"I'm all right. Shifu, my mother is in the Magistrate's prison. Did you know that too?"

"The prison?" Shifu stood still as if to absorb a blow. Then his wisps of hair waved left and right. "What, writing letters is illegal? And she has no arm! No arm ... she can't even do it anymore!"

"The Magistrate fears rebels," said Zun.

"Oh ... well, his strategy is poor. Washing a hand to clean his foot!"

"Ma said that we don't really know – "

"Wait!" Shifu held up his hand. "Wang Zun," he looked her directly in the eye. "Sit, please. Rest and eat, before anything else. Do you like wet food, or dry food? We made both today."

He waved her to the table and put a big bowl in front of her. It contained a steaming soup, filled with many kinds of mountain roots and vegetables, and fresh noodles. Across the table, roasted yams released sweet, warm steam when Shifu cut them open. Zun drooled and quickly wiped her mouth, hoping no one noticed.

"Everyone, eat," said Shifu, and Zun took a sip from her bowl. More delicious than the taste was the warmth that spread through her middle. Shifu and the boys acted as if they were just as famished as she was, and no one spoke for a while as they shoveled in food. Shifu refilled Zun's bowl until she begged him to stop. Finally he put down his chopsticks.

"Boys, get quilts for Wang Zun."

"Will he sleep with us?" asked Han.

"No, Wang Zun is a girl. She will sleep in here. We'll sleep in the back room."

The boys' eyes slid and locked on Zun's chest. She still wore the heavy, loose workman's jacket that Zhang Ayi had given her. Her cheeks burned. Uncouth males were the same everywhere. Suddenly she felt that the whole idea of coming here was stupid. She was a stranger to these people. She couldn't sit here and accept their food and hospitality. She'd owe them, and she had no way to pay.

"Get the bedding!" urged Shifu. The boys scattered. "Wang Zun, help me clear the table," he said to her.

She stood up. "Shifu, thank you very much for the meal, and please don't put the bedding out. I can sleep on the floor. Tomorrow morning I can gather wood for you or do some work in exchange for my food, and then I'll leave." She bowed. "Thank you," she repeated.

"Very good, very good," Shifu said. "Wang Zun, did you know I once taught your father Wang Fei, in Shanghai? He was my student in the martial arts."

"My father, your student? He learned wu shu?" Zun tried to remember if she had ever seen her father fighting. "I don't think you taught him very well," she said without thinking.

"No, I don't think I did," Shifu admitted, nodding his head.

"You could've taught my father to defend himself," said Zun.

"Yes," Shifu said simply. "Did he tell you about his days as a wu shu student?"

Zun shook her head.

"Please sit, Wang Zun." She sat, and he joined her. The boys came back in the room with quilts and he motioned the boys to sit down with them. "He was a decent student. Tell him to stand, and he'd stand. Tell him to strike, and he'd strike. He followed our discipline. But he was happiest when something broke. When our pump split and overflowed, he fixed it. He made us clever drums and gongs. He fixed our wheelbarrow. If you sent him to the market, he spent hours examining all the toys and puzzles. Shanghai has many foreigners, and rich men who buy foreign machines – lamps with trapped lightning, clocks with moving dolls, big smoking engines, and of course bicycles – those are two-wheeled carts that you straddle and propel with your feet," he said to Han and Li.

"A few years after Wang Fei joined us, he came back very excited. He got a job taking care of Lord An's machines. He gave up wu shu but he came back to visit. We didn't see each other often, but I heard he went to Wanzhou and got married. Years later, I was travelling in some hills near Wanzhou – and, well, after many adventures, I rescued Li and Han here. They were little babies, the only survivors of Hing village, which was burned to the ground.

"I had no idea how to take care of babies, and no milk to give them. I found my old student Feng, who had ten children, but he would not take two more. I always thought his stances were a little tight. Then I went to Wang Fei. You were just a little baby, Wang Zun. Wang Fei said his wife was already very tired. But I begged for help to feed the boys. Chen Ru Lin, your mother, came out and said, 'I'll feed them, if you bring me fried chicken.'

"So, I hauled wheelbarrows to make money for Chen Ru Lin's fried chicken. She ate like five warriors but became as thin as a twig, feeding three babies."

Zun squirmed in her chair and glanced at the boys. They stared at the floor. *Ma fed them?* Ma was so proud of being able to read classical Chinese script and earning money for the family. It was shocking to think she had spent months as a wet nurse. For three children!

"This Chen Ru Lin who fed us – is she the one in prison now?" asked Li.

"Aren't you paying attention?" sputtered Han.

"I wanted to be certain," said Li.

"Yes, Chen Ru Lin is the one. She did much more than feed you. It was very difficult for her, you know. She could comfort you like no one else, and you all wanted her. Imagine making one baby happy, and then two more are waiting! But it was all over too soon.

"When you three were about a year old, some evil nuns recognized me in the marketplace. Another long story. I knew I had to leave town." The old man compressed his lips in thought.

"You boys would probably have been safe with Wang Fei and Chen Ru Lin. But I would always worry if those who burned Hing village would come after you. So we hid, and moved from place to place. My older sister Yang Jie brings us news. That's how I knew, Wang Zun – about your father."

The three twelve-year-olds shifted in their seats, trying to understand what they had heard.

"Evil nuns," said Han.

"Not all nuns are evil," said Zun. "Who burned the village? Was it the Magistrate?"

"Could have been bandits," said Shifu. "But that village was one of several in the mountains that hauled gravel for the Magistrate's new buildings. They were forced to sell the gravel at a fixed price that was very low. The case was never solved. And now we're here, and it's time to rest. Go on, boys, you know what to do."

"Shifu, we'll go to the city and rescue Wang Zun's mother and avenge our village?" asked Han, with bright eyes.

"I meant, it's time to brush your teeth!" cried Shifu.

"But Shifu, this is a moment of destiny, isn't it?" protested Li. "This is what we have trained for all our lives – "

"Don't undo your years of training with bad sleep and foul teeth," snapped Shifu. "I'll give Wang Zun a choice before bed. Song or story?"

"STORY!" screamed the boys.

"I said Wang Zun's choice!" thundered Shifu.

"Story," murmured Zun.

Shifu nodded. He told them about Eternal Student Pao who searched the world for the best teacher; little Yin Qi, who was born with no fingers but perfected the inimitable Wrist Whip; and Song Yang Rong Qu, who saved her parents' rice farm by defeating both armies warring over it. As soon as he was done, Han and Li clamored for more.

"Wang Zun has only heard three," said Li.

"She needs to rest! You two, go and clean up," ordered Shifu.

The boys went to the kitchen area and began to brush their teeth. Shifu gave Zun a new toothbrush, a nice one with meticulously trimmed bristles. Where did he get such bristles, in the middle of the forest? She suddenly remembered the big black and white pig and put the brush on the counter.

Shifu gave her a chamber pot and spoke softly.

"How is Wang Zun's excrement?"

Zun did not know how to answer this question, but Shifu looked expectant. "Nothing to complain about," she said.

"Should be better now you've had a decent meal. Sleep well!"

Zun had no idea what awaited her as she slid into the little bed in the corner. The sheets smelled faintly of soap, reassuring but not overpowering, and the cotton-stuffed mattress gave her stiff back a little hug. The quilt was heavy and thick enough to make her feel safe, like an animal in a burrow. For the first time in many days, she dropped right off to sleep.

The next morning she woke to a chorus of tooth brushing, spitting, and phlegm-clearing from the next room. She curled deeper under her quilt, but changed her mind and jumped out. Maybe, if Shifu were indebted to Ma, he'd come back to Wanzhou and help rescue her. The connecting door to the other room opened and Han's tufted head popped out.

"You're up," he said. "Coming through to get water." And he stepped inside the kitchen, grabbed two wooden buckets, and went out. Through the open door Zun could see Shifu sitting cross-legged on the floor with her jacket. He held up the needle he was using.

"Shifu mends jackets very quickly!" He resumed sewing with great concentration. Li ran past him through the door and out of the house. "Ah," Shifu said, looking after Li. "Before breakfast, the boys do breathing exercises. Wang Zun, you're welcome to join us. There is much to do later: dry bean curd, gather berries, gather wood, enough to last the winter!" He neatly folded Zun's jacket and followed Li out.

Zun tried to understand what Shifu had just said. What did he mean, the winter? Did he think she would simply stay in the woods, while Ma was in the Magistrate's prison?

In the back yard behind the little house, Han, Li and the big pig waited in a straight row. Shifu stood before them. Of course, this is when they'd practice their martial arts. Zun would practice too. She had to be ready to face the Magistrate's army.

Shifu spread his arms out in a circle and inhaled. He brought his arms down and exhaled, and proceeded to bend and stretch. The boys followed Shifu's moves exactly, while the pig did what he could and occasionally added some tail stretches and ear swishes. Zun did her best to follow. Then Shifu took a deep breath and sank into his meditative stance – the horse stance – arms straight out, legs apart and bent at the knee to form a rectangle, back straight. The boys followed. The pig balanced on his left front and right rear trotters.

Zun imitated their form. This was easy! But within seconds her leg muscles began to burn. *I've been walking for days; I can do this*, she thought. *Those boys can do it.* Slowly her shaking thighs inched up, and her behind stuck out. She locked herself in a painful crouch. It was excruciating. Shifu and the boys had their eyes closed.

"Shifu, I've been thinking," she said calmly, "We are only four days from the city. We can carry enough food to last us that long – I'm sorry I have no money – and then we can rescue my mother. After that, you can come back here to the hills." Her knees shook.

Shifu sank a fraction lower in his stance and said not a word.

Zun waited. The morning sun that felt so light and cool began to carry a burning knife. A stray hair tickled her eyes.

"Ha!" Shifu shouted, and savagely knuckle-punched the air.

"Ha!" the boys shouted back. "Ha! Ha!" With each shout they jumped, twisted, and knuckle-punched a different direction.

Shifu walked around them making minor adjustments to their form as Zun watched.

When Shifu paused, Zun said, "Shifu, did you hear what I – "

"HO!" shouted Shifu and jumped into his knuckle punch.

"Ho," said Zun, imitating him. It was impossible somehow not to follow.

After a long series of knuckle punches, Shifu made them bend and stretch.

As they finally slowed down, Zun felt as weak and wobbly as a baby. *Which is what he wants*, she thought. *He's worse than Ba and Ma. He can treat these boys like infants, but not me. This is a waste of time. I'm getting out of here.*

"Wang Zun! Let's go inside. I have the best bean-curd pickle for your porridge!"

9. The Bean Curd Rebellion

Bean-curd pickle indeed. She followed Shifu as he lit a handful of grass for his stove.

"Shifu, my mother said to come to you, and that's why I'm here. But you can't keep me. I came for help to rescue my mother, and if you won't, I'll go do it myself."

Shifu sighed. "Wang Zun, you're not going anywhere. Your parents long knew they were in danger. And I promised them I would care for you if anything happened to them."

"I don't believe you!" blurted Zun. She couldn't face the idea that her parents made an agreement with this old man about her, without telling her.

There was silence in the room at her outburst. The boys were watching with great interest. She wanted to hurl the pot of porridge at them. "What are you looking at?"

"Wait here, Wang Zun." Shifu went to the other room and returned with a piece of paper.

It was a letter in Ma's handwriting. The date was four years ago.

Honored Shifu,

We hope you are well. The Government constables have arrested many people, but we are safe. Wang Fei is working at the loading docks for now. Little Zun is as tall as my shoulder. I can't write more, but send warm regards to you and Hing Han and Hing Li. If those evil melon-heads come after you, remember we'll take care of the boys, just as you would our Zun.

Chen Ru Lin

Then it was true. Ma had sent her here to hide with Shifu and the boys.

"Who are the evil melon-heads?"

"Oh, that's just your mother's way of talking. You get the gist of the letter."

"Well, not entirely. What kind of danger were Ma and Ba in?"

"Wang Zun, I can't answer all your questions. But I can tell you why we made our plan to take care of you." Shifu sighed. "See the date on this letter? 1898. Do you know about the Hundred Days' Reform?"

Zun shook her head. Li stood up.

"Well, you were so young, only eight years old," muttered Shifu. "Li, sit down. How about the Taiping Rebellion?"

Zun nodded. Li stood up.

"Nien Rebellion? Du Wenxiu Rebellion? Well then, you know the Qing Empire has had many rebellions to deal with in the last fifty years. Li, please stay seated. I'll call on you if I need to."

"*Know–it–all!*" hissed Han at Li.

"*Monkey!*" Li hissed back.

"Were Ma and Ba rebels?" Zun persisted.

"No, of course not, no. You see the Imperial Government itches all over with rebellions, and it doesn't even know where to scratch itself. It lashes out like a dog with too many fleas. Anyone who does things a little differently makes the dog turn and snap."

"Hmm," nodded Zun.

"And then there are the foreigners. Two years ago, the Empress supported an uprising against the foreigners in Beijing. A few hundred foreigners were killed, and thousands of Chinese – Chinese who supported the foreigners, and Chinese who fought against the foreigners."

"Ma and Ba aren't foreigners!"

"No, but the Empress is afraid of foreigners – and foreign ideas."

Zun nodded.

"For two thousand years," he continued, 'the Chinese Empire withstood famines and floods, infighting and invasions. But now it's weak, and foreigners are numerous and powerful. Many people, even some inside the Imperial Government, want changes. In 1898, they drafted the Hundred Days' Reform. They said, 'Let's train officials in science as well as poetry. Let's have schools for boys *and* girls. Let's distribute food to the hungry, and build roads.' It was very exciting."

"1898 – that was when Ba's brother delivered the bicycle from Shanghai," said Zun. "Did they really do all that in a hundred days?"

"No. After only a hundred days, the Empress put a stop to it. She decreed death for the scholars who drafted the reform."

"What does this have to do with my parents?"

"Lord An – the man who gave your father the bicycle – was one of the scholars she executed."

The bicycle. Zun remembered that last afternoon with Ba, in the courtyard, the way Ba and Ma talked about meeting the businessmen, about the bicycle factory, the way they hid things from her.

"I saw my parents being careful," she said, and the words hung in the air.

Han nudged Shifu's elbow. "Shifu, I really don't understand the part about this bicycle."

"Wang Zun knows. Please tell the boys about it," said Shifu.

She looked at the two expectant faces of the boys. "A bicycle is a two-wheeled cart that you propel with your feet," she began. "It goes as fast as a horse, but you don't have to feed it – "

"And it doesn't heap filth on the streets!" added Shifu.

The boys looked eager to know more.

She put two plates side by side on the table, and held them on their rims, like bicycle wheels. "A metal frame holds the wheels together, and you sit astride the frame on a seat. Your feet push cranks in a circle, and the cranks turn one of the wheels. There are handlebars to steer the front wheel. Have you ever seen an old-fashioned bicycle, with the big wheel in front and the small wheel behind?"

The boys shook their heads.

"Our bicycle is a new design. Instead of using a giant wheel connected to the crank, we have the crank connected to a gear that pulls a chain."

She took the original two same-sized plates, for the bicycle wheels, and placed the spoon in between them, where the pedal crank would be. Under the spoon, she placed a small plate.

"See, this small plate is the gear that rotates with the crank." She pulled out a long black hair from her head and arranged it around the small plate, and placed another smaller plate on top of the rear wheel-plate. She wound the black hair around the first small plate and the second smaller plate.

"This hair is the chain. If I turn the crank, the first plate turns. It pulls the chain, and the chain turns the second plate, and that turns the wheel. With these different-sized gears, you get the same power you get with a big wheel, but in a more compact form!" She turned the spoon and the small gear-plate together with one hand, and turned the smaller gear plate with the other. "If the rear gear is half the size of the front gear, then one turn of the front gear corresponds to two turns of the back gear; two turns of the bicycle wheel equals one turn of the pedals."

The boys watched in awe.

"So those French people invented a way to turn the feet to turn the gears and turn the wheel. Fascinating," said Li.

Han mouthed *know-it-all* at him.

"But here's my favorite thing," Zun continued. "The freewheel. It's a part on the hub of the driving wheel that lets your feet take a rest. The bicycle moves even if your feet stop turning the cranks. So you can push, push, push, and then glide. Or go down a hill without moving anything. It's fun! It's like flying!"

"What if you roll down the hill too fast?" asked Han in alarm.

"You use the brake. It's another metal part attached to the wheel. Our bicycle has a rear brake. My father designed a brake for the front wheel."

"I'd like to ride a machine like that," said Li.

Zun felt a warmth rise in her. It was a strange kind of pleasure to tell them about Ba's work. She never felt such pure pride. It was a joyous, cutting feeling that brought tears which she quickly brushed with her sleeve.

"Shifu, this girl is more interesting than I thought," said Han.

"Han, how rude! She's sitting right here! You mustn't talk about people like that," said Shifu.

Zun's moment of happiness evaporated.

"Enough talking! We haven't even had breakfast."

Aiya, breakfast and cleaning and phlegm! "But my mother – " began Zun.

"Please help make breakfast."

"No! My mother!" Zun was so frustrated she couldn't finish her sentence.

"Wang Zun," said Shifu, softly. "Your mother is a great friend of mine. I'll do all I can to rescue her. But I must think, and plan. For now, help me steam this fish. Li, get more wood."

Zun complied and chopped ginger. She thought of Ma in the Magistrate's compound. She imagined many servants toiling like she was in the Magistrate's kitchen, maybe at the very same moment. If only she could switch places with them! An idea formed in her head.

She could get work as a servant in the Magistrate's compound. She would obey and work hard, and learn the path to the dungeon. Why didn't she think of this before? She wondered what Shifu would have to say about this.

"Shifu, what do you think is the best way for us to get Ma out of the dungeon?"

"Eh? Is Li back from getting wood?" Shifu muttered while he chopped green onions.

He had not been thinking about Ma at all! Zun felt her cheeks grow hot. *Maybe this old man is the wrong kind of Shifu, a Shifu of household chores. Maybe he could rescue bits of food stuck in his teeth, but not a woman in a dungeon. And those boys – why do they call him Shifu? In all respects, he behaves like their father. They're just weird.* The words of the poem from the Consort came to her mind:

To no one can I speak
For who can understand me?
...
What good is the heart of a hero
Beneath my dress?

Whatever Shifu said, she was leaving. She must go back to the city. But it was Han who spoke up from a bowl of ground bean paste. "Shifu, when will we leave for the city?" he asked.

"What? You're not going to the city!"

"We must rescue Wang Zun's mother! And avenge the massacre of our village!"

Shifu froze in the middle of sliding green onions on top of the fish in the steamer, caught between the gaze of Han and Zun. "What now, you two," he said, and finished with the onions. "Neither of you is going to the city. I thought I was clear. It's much too dangerous. You'll stay here, with Pig-Pig."

"But you said we'd go to the city eventually! Why not now?" protested Han.

"I expect you to live long enough to finish your education! It's time to start learning the violin. And you haven't even finished the Invisible Squirrel."

The old man was back to treating them all like little children again.

Zun enunciated like a chisel on ice: "Honored Shifu, with all due respect, my own personal filial duty is of the highest – "

Li swung the front door open. An old half-bald crow sat on his shoulder and uttered a long cry followed by a short croak. "Armed men approaching!" hissed Li. "On horseback!" The bird scraped his shoulder gently. "Fifty of them!"

10. The Horizontal Journey

"Wang Zun! Go with Pig-Pig! We meet at the half-twist tree," ordered Shifu. "Han, Li, stay with me. Get the weapons, and some ropes!" Han still clutched the bean bowl, fingers tense. Shifu cast an arm around his shoulders and smiled. "Today we finish the Invisible Squirrel." He stepped to the front door and called out, "Pig-Pig! Come here!"

Pig-Pig trotted into the house. Shifu scratched Pig-Pig's chin, and beckoned Zun over. He picked up a lower corner of Zun's jacket. He rubbed his hand on the jacket. "Half-twist tree," Shifu repeated.

Pig-Pig grunted and started out the door, stopping to look at Zun. She ran for her sack, and followed Pig-Pig out the back. She stopped to look back at the little house where she had had a moment's relief from her lonely journey. Awash in the bright noonday light it looked small and ordinary. Smoke rose from the chimney; the half-bald crow landed on Li in a tree on the left, and Han silently climbed a tree on the right. She could still smell their uneaten steamed fish and rice.

She heard horsemen approach the front of the house. She slipped around the side of the house; she had to see. They wore the armor of Wanzhou government soldiers, like the one she had seen on the street on her last ride with Ba. Dread gripped her. This could end badly.

Shifu pulled weeds in the front yard.

The lead soldier brandished a spear. Many riders drew arrows.

"Old Man, we're following a rebel," said the leader, pointing a spear at Shifu.

Shifu pretended to slowly straighten his old back. "No rebels here, young grandson. And please keep your horses away from my winter cabbages. May I offer you some nice, wholesome – "

"Take him," muttered the commander to another soldier, and he moved his horse and spear forward. The archers trained their arrows on Shifu.

The crow flapped and screamed on one side, and Han threw, at lightning speed, five metal darts at the archers. They shot, but their arrows went wild. A burning arrow hit the roof.

Shifu jumped from the mulberry stump to the fence post. The leader twisted in his saddle to thrust his spear at the old man, but Shifu grabbed the spear and poked back, pushing the lead soldier off his horse.

Han unsheathed two glistening daggers, and Zun – and all the soldiers – watched in amazement as he jumped and did a no-handed cartwheel along a horizontal branch of the tree, landing with perfect balance. A flurry of arrows followed him – he was a clear target! He flicked and swung his dual blades so that every deadly arrow glanced aside.

A man's yelp below rang with surprise and pain. The tip of Li's staff waved sided to side as he ran silently through the ranks of the archers, knocking the bows from their arms. Li turned and pushed the staff through a join in a soldier's armor; the man grabbed at his side and fell off his horse.

Mounted soldiers wheeled and brought out spears, swords, and daggers. Armor clanked and shifted; weapons clinked and thrust. Zun couldn't move. She imagined this must be how it had been, the night of Ba's death.

Shifu fought off a ring of horsemen with the downed leader's spear. Freckles and wisps of hair seemed to fade – the fussy hen had turned into a man. As Zun watched, stricken, forced to relive the terror of the murderous attack against her family, Shifu transformed the fight. The flashing tip of his spear blighted every soldier's attack. He turned their heavy, killing march into a wild dance they stumbled to follow.

Oh, if I could do that … if only I had learned to do that …

Han dropped into the space with Shifu and they fought together, back to back.

But in the ranks behind them, soldiers were frantically struggling with something – taking things from their bags and pouches. Zun stood up.

"Guns!" she cried. She didn't know what kind of guns they had – rifles or muskets. She knew they were dangerous and that no person could outmaneuver a bullet.

Shifu and Han jumped up into the air – and did not come back down. Where did they go?

The soldiers lifted their guns to their shoulders, and searched for a target. Li had just swept his staff at a soldier's legs and knocked him down.

Zun gasped, "Li!" But just as she said it, a gun-holding soldier lurched forward as he was pushed sharply from behind. He dropped the gun and scrambled to regain his balance, as the next soldier was pushed, and then another. Something pushed the first two soldiers off their horses, and Han jumped up from behind to fight them. He landed in a powerful crouch, his two hands cupped, as if they held the top and bottom of a giant, invisible acorn.

He held the pose for only an instant, as Shifu and Li joined him, starting from the same stance.

Zun choked as she realized – *it's the stance of the Squirrel!*

Behind the ten or twenty soldiers she was able to see, a bristle of weapons encroached. Shots rang out. The boys and Shifu fought well, but far too many soldiers were coming. Zun was still unable to move. Pig-Pig came and pulled the edge of her jacket with his teeth, but she held on to the tree beside her. She couldn't leave Shifu.

"Han, now!" he cried.

Han lifted a dagger to his shoulder and threw it into the trees. With a hissing, whipping sound, a huge twisted-rope net, as long and as wide as a house, fell on the approaching soldiers. There was a terrific noise as the men yelled and the horses screamed. A few straggling soldiers untouched by the net wheeled and rode away. The trapped soldiers lost their balance and fell off their horses; they hacked at the net with their swords and spears. Surely the net would not hold them for long.

Shifu and the boys ignored the net entirely. They battled the remaining soldiers.

The noises from the net subsided. The hacking and flailing stopped. The horses and soldiers seemed to all fall down dead under it.

Li pointed his staff at them and raised his eyebrows at Shifu, but Shifu shook his head. "Make sure that the ones left here are well tied up!"

The lead soldier in the front yard shook his head and got up off the ground, unnoticed. He looked around the house and saw Zun staring at him from the trees. He lifted his wrist, and she turned and ran into the woods. She felt a sting in her back, and kept running. A tingling pain snaked around her ribs.

She stumbled and caught herself, and kept going into the woods.

Footsteps came closer and closer.

"Wang Zun, stop!" hissed Shifu behind her.

She stumbled and slowed, and he held her shoulders and examined her back.

"You've been hit. *Aiya*, there's a dart." He bent his head to smell the dart. "Poison. Come back to the clearing."

Poison! Did this mean she would die? "Get it off me! Take it out!" She flailed at her back.

"Calm down, don't get all excited! I've seen these before."

"Will I die, like those soldiers under the net?"

"Under the net? Of course not, *urrh*," Shifu cleared his throat. "I put something in the net to make them sleep. They'll wake up later and get out."

The cottage roof was aflame. Groups of soldiers were tied to fence posts and trees. Han and Li frantically sloshed buckets of water at the roof.

Shifu made Zun lie on her stomach. "I ask your pardon, Wang Zun," he said, and lifted her jacket and shirt. He removed the dart, and sucked the wound and spat, sucked and spat, several times.

"Han, water, soap!" He looked around for the leader of the soldiers. "Did you make this poison? Do you have an antidote?"

The leader sat cross-legged on the ground with his hands tied behind him. He glanced at Zun. "*That's* the rebel? He's just a kid. Save your worry. He's dead."

Zun squirmed.

"Don't listen to him, and don't move," Shifu said to her. He ran to the soldier and searched his pockets. But he found nothing.

"Li, Han – come here. Get the scrolls, weapons, whatever food you can carry. Let the house burn. Go!"

"But we can save it!" Li cried.

"No, we must leave. The soldiers who escaped will come back with more men. Wang Zun is poisoned. We must go!"

The boys dropped their buckets and stared.

Zun lifted her head and shoulders, "Shifu, I'm sorry – "

"Stay still! Do not let the poison circulate," snapped Shifu. He had not used that tone with her before.

The old man ran with the boys into the house. Zun put down her head and felt miserable. She didn't know if it was the poison or the smoke, but her head swam. And the soldiers were looking for *rebels from Wanzhou* – they must have followed her here. It was her fault Shifu's home was destroyed.

He ran out with two long poles and a sheet. He placed the two poles parallel to one another, an arm's width apart, and tied the sheet over the poles to make a litter.

They lifted Zun onto the litter. Two at a time, they took turns carrying Zun through the woods.

Lying on her stomach, Zun could see little. She heard soft grunts from Pig-Pig just ahead, and the swish of weeds and bushes as they brushed past them. Every twenty minutes or so, they put her down and traded positions. The litter sometimes jerked and bumped as they went over the uneven ground. She did not mind at first, but then the cramping began. Her stomach seized and churned painfully, and under the warm afternoon sun her face beaded in cold sweat. When at last they stopped for a break and lowered the litter to the ground, Shifu checked on her.

He looked worried. "Wang Zun, how do you feel?"

She nodded her head, but felt a sharp cramp again and her back curved up.

"What is it? Your stomach?"

She nodded again. He helped her into a side position where she could curl up her legs to relieve the pain, and wiped her face. He jumped up.

"Let's go, Pig-Pig. Come, boys! Boys, where are you?" They had wandered off.

Han and Li returned, shame-faced. "Just resting a little, Shifu," said Li.

"We must go faster. Wang Zun is not well. Always stay where I can see you!"

Han picked up a bulging sack and Li took his turn at the front of the litter. Shifu took the other set of handles, and kept an eye on Zun.

Aiya, thought Zun. *Shifu is still mad. They must all hate me.*

With every lurch of the litter, her pain-wracked torso tightened. Shifu and the boys hurried, so they bumped more than before. Night fell. "Try to rest, Wang Zun," said Shifu, and pressed some places on her head with his fingers. "Think of a beautiful place," he added.

She thought of last spring. Tramping through thick mud – the plum orchards east of town, after rain. She smelled the blossoms before she saw them, for Ba had made her close her eyes. *"Don't open, not yet ... now!"* And she was in a riot of flowers, the air so clear she could distinguish every petal, a splash of white tinged with pink.

But she'll never go there again, not with Ba gone. Tears made a chafing puddle in the cloth of her litter. She was about to die here anyway.

"Shifu," said Li, panting a little. "Don't you think Han finished today?" Li and Shifu were carrying Zun, and Han was alongside, loaded with swords and food.

"What? Be quiet, save your strength. I don't know what you're talking about."

"The Invisible Squirrel. Did he pass the test?"

Han kicked along, pretending to take no notice.

"Oh," Shifu chuckled. "Yes, he did. Today, Han, you finished. Congratulations!"

Even in the growing darkness, Han's grin was brilliant.

"I mean it now, though. Be quiet. Wang Zun must rest."

What would Ba do, if he'd seen the Invisible Squirrel? He'd be overjoyed. "Excellent!" he'd cry, and throw his arm around their shoulders, and clap, and make bad poetry to praise them. And he'd be grateful to them for working so hard to save her. If he were lying on this litter, he'd be chatting, to cheer everyone up, until they ordered him to stop.

So, she must go back to the plum trees. They were beautiful all year long. The cramping eased off a bit and she dozed.

***

"Her eyes are open! Give her some fish," came Han's voice. But Zun did not want to eat; her teeth chattered.

"She's too cold. She hasn't been moving." Shifu covered her with his warm jacket. "We can't afford to stop."

They forded a small stream, and her stomach got wet. The horrible cramps began again.

At dawn they reached the shores of a wide river. The boys gently laid the litter on the bank, and rubbed their palms. She heard the sound of small waves and with effort lifted her head to see. The light off the water hurt her eyes. It was empty as far as she could see: no boats, no people.

"Hei Yisheng – Dr. Hei – where are you," Shifu murmured.

"I'm so cold," Zun could not help saying. She tried to curl up her knees. "I can't move my legs!"

Shifu took the boys aside and spoke softly to them. But she could hear.

"I know you're tired. But we have to go on. Now that she can't move her legs, it's dangerous. We must keep her awake. If she doesn't get an antidote soon – " he didn't finish.

Han said, "Shifu, which way do we go, upriver or down?"

"I don't know. We need to find people and ask for Hei Yisheng."

Shifu took up the two rear litter poles, and Han and Li scrambled for the front two poles. "Pig-Pig!" said Shifu. "Find people! Smell some people!"

Pig-Pig sniffed, and darted downriver. They scurried after him.

A thick mist settled on the bank. The ground became wet and marshy. Zun lay curled like a cooked shrimp in the litter. Everything hurt. Her stomach cramped, and the heavy, wet smell of the river mud pained her head.

"Shifu, look!" Li pointed. A shadow bobbed in the mist over the water: a barge. They put Zun down in the driest spot they could find, and shouted and waved.

A woman stepped out on the stern of the barge and stared at them.

"I'm looking for Hei Yisheng!" Shifu shouted.

"She's not here!" the woman turned to go back inside her barge.

"I need Hei Yisheng immediately! Where is she?"

The woman stopped on her deck, but did not say anything.

"I'll give you one and a half taels!"

The woman looked up.

"Two taels, and no more!"

The woman threw a rope at them, and they towed the barge to shore. She pocketed Shifu's coins, looked at Zun prone on the litter, and said, "Hei Yisheng is up the Ling canal. About eight *li* from here."

"Did Hei Yisheng give you any medicine? Do you still have it?" asked Shifu.

"Yes," said the woman.

"Thank you," said Shifu. "Boys, I think it would be faster to fetch her here. Give me some paper and a brush." Shifu wrote a note, and wrapped it around the dart he had removed from Zun's back. He fastened the package around Pig-Pig's neck.

"She won't come for *you*," said the barge woman. "She hasn't come for anyone in months. She stopped talking to people when – "

"Bring me the medicine she gave you," said Shifu.

"Absolutely not! It is mine!"

"I just want the pig to smell it. That way he can find her," he said. "I won't keep it, on my word as teacher of wu shu."

Zun rolled her head and tried to breathe. Her chest hurt.

The barge woman gave her a once-over. "Put your mind at ease. I have some coffins for sale."

"Quiet!" Shifu shouted. "Get me the medicine. I gave you two taels!"

Zun cringed at his voice. If he is shouting like that, the woman must be close to the truth. She began to cry.

"I'll escort you to your boat," Shifu said to the woman. "Boys, stay with Wang Zun! Don't let her sleep!"

A tufted shadow blotted the misty light over her face.

"Don't worry, Hei Yisheng's medicine is very good," Han stood over her.

"Pig-Pig can run eight *li* in a few minutes, you'll see," said Li.

"I'm very sorry you lost your home," Zun choked out. "Please know I did not intend – "

"Oh, we move every year," said Li.

"We want to live in the city," said Han. "It'll all work out. I know! Shifu will take care of you, and you can marry one of us. Maybe Li. And then you have nothing to worry about. All taken care of."

"Either way, but probably Han would make a better husband," said Li. "If you think about it – "

Zun grabbed the edge of the litter, lifted her body forward on her elbows, and vomited onto the grass. When she was done, the boys gently slid her back onto the litter and moved her to clean ground.

"Li, watch what you say," said Han, frowning at him.

"*You* watch it," said Li.

"Han! Get over here!" shouted Shifu. "Pig-Pig has the scent! Run with him!"

Shifu brought boiled water and wet Zun's dry lips and tongue. "Shall I sing?"

She shook her head.

"Story?"

Again, she shook her head. Wave upon wave of the cramps kept coming, and she felt it was all she could do to get through each one.

"Li, help me move her to the shade."

The brown winter grass twitched slightly in front of her face. The blades of grass became dim and smeared together.

"Wang Zun, Wang Zun! You mustn't sleep." Now Shifu shook her head.

Zun felt a wave of irritation. *Who is this old man, spitting on my face? And what's he so excited about?*

"Wang Zun, if you fall asleep now you won't wake up! Listen to me, don't you want to see your mother?"

Ma! Where's Ma? Oh, that's who this old man is – "You listen, you Magistrate, release my mother!" She reached her hands into the dirt, trying to prop herself up.

"What?"

"I said, Magistrate, release my mother. She's not a rebel!"

"Oh, but, hmm. Hmm. I have evidence that she's a rebel."

"What evidence?"

"I have eleven pieces of evidence. If you refute each one, I might consider releasing your mother."

Zun struggled to sit up.

"Do not rise in my presence! Pay attention," commanded Shifu. "The first piece of evidence is her shoes."

"What?" Zun struggled to concentrate.

"Rebel shoes, I can smell them. Go on. Prove me wrong."

11. The Green Purse

She was lurching. *Make it stop*. She closed her eyes to make it go away. But it got much worse; she felt a cold drifting, and a ring of cold clamped around her neck. A wave sloshed water up her nose and she sputtered. She opened her eyes to cruel bright light that shimmered everywhere. She was in the water! The crazy old man had carried her into the water!

"Wang Zun! Do you hear me?"

His wisps of beard streamed with droplets.

Zun could hear him, but answering just didn't matter. The cruel light and the cold water didn't matter either. She was just going to drift away.

"Your mother, Wang Zun, think of your mother!"

"Ma?" Zun opened her eyes a fraction and looked around. "Ma?" Oh yes, there were eleven ridiculous charges against her. Her shoes, the fact that she could read – that made no sense, the Consort could read; surely it wasn't rebellious to read – the shape of her eyebrows, a mole on her ear, secret rebel letters. *Did Ma write secret letters?*

Where was Ma? Zun could hear some kind of shouting, but didn't pay attention anymore. She hurt all over, and it was difficult to breathe enough. She couldn't get enough air. *Ma*, she thought. *I'm coming for you.*

She clung to that thought, even while there was more shouting, and lurching up and down, and strange sensations popped all over her body, feelings of being poked and pricked. A shivering warmth spread through her and she opened her eyes.

She lay in the shade on the dried mud of the canal bank. She lifted her head, and saw that she was only in her underclothes. Her arms and legs, all her exposed skin, were covered with needles!

"She's awake," said a husky voice.

An enormous woman knelt beside her. Her folded knee towered above Zun's shoulder. Her huge face and her unbound, wiry, mist-soaked hair made her head seem like a mountain. Most unsettling were her nostrils, sharply round and densely black. Zun gasped.

Shifu ran over. At the sight of Zun's underclothes he turned his head. "It's all right, Wang Zun, this is Hei Yisheng – Dr. Hei."

"Don't call me a doctor. I'm just Hei," said the large woman. She felt Zun's pulse. "Hmm. Mm. This is not a happy liver." She peered into Zun's face. "You vomited?"

Zun could only part her lips in reply.

"Don't move. Inhale this," said Hei, holding a smelly yellow lump before Zun's nose. "Don't touch it. Just inhale the fumes. Now swallow," Hei lifted Zun's head and nudged a small cup of heavy liquid to her lips. Zun felt it slither down her throat.

"Try to rest," said Hei. "I'll move the needles."

Strange pulses drifted from the needles as Hei twisted and jiggled them in a hither-thither pattern on her body, as if Zun were a musical instrument.

Maybe she's playing some kind of demon song. The vibration from the needles seemed to reach the medicine in her stomach. It felt like the medicine turned into a wiggling tadpole, and then a deliberate frog. Hei sat alongside Zun and nodded as if she knew all about the frog. Zun wanted to ask her, but there was something wrong. Zun counted three nostrils in Hei's nose: left, right, and horrible center. She felt she could almost see the air being sucked into that dark nostril.

A bell tinkled – a sweet silver bell. Zun woke.

The real Hei, the two-nostril one, held a little bell and rang it. The sky behind her was dusky grey. The harsh light was gone. The needles were gone.

Zun breathed deep. She was happy to breathe like that again. With each breath, she felt her mists of confusion sweep away. There was no frog in her stomach. The woman Hei had a normal nose. The Magistrate was far away, back in the city. Zun must go back and rescue Ma.

She tried to sit up, but was too weak.

Hei put an arm behind her. "You must lie back and rest. Drink some water," she said.

"But I'll be all right now, won't I?"

Hei nodded. "I recommend you avoid poison darts in the future. Here, let's get you dressed." Hei helped her with her tunic and jacket.

"Thank you very much, Hei Yisheng!"

"Hei. Just Hei. I didn't do much. The reason you're alive, little girl, is that the *amateur*," she pushed out her lips in repugnance, 'the amateur who concocted that poison did not decant the metallic humors at the correct pressure. If it were my brew, you'd have been stiff, blue, and dead in five minutes. Shifu did well to suck out most of it. Me – I take little credit."

"Hei Yisheng! Hei Yisheng!" The woman from the barge ran to them. "You came – "

"And now I must be going," said Hei. "Hut-hut-hut!" A long-legged camel trotted to the canal bank. Zun stared. She'd never seen a camel so close before. It had tall knobbed knees, big round feet, and a scruffy hump. It yawned, slime stringing between its teeth. She cringed at its horrible breath.

"Bas, bas." Hei strode over to the camel and patted its neck.

"Please," the barge woman continued, 'come see my old father. His back aches again. And my daughter wheezes in the night. Please!"

Hei bent her head. "For that there are many healers better than me," she mumbled. She got on her camel and her broad back swayed a definite goodbye.

"How did you get her to come here?" whispered the barge woman to Shifu. "She hasn't left her barge for six months. Not since her husband died."

The words lifted Zun's feet. Still dizzy from her cure from the poison, she ran after Hei. "Hei Yisheng, stay and help these people! You saved *me* – " Zun tripped on grassy stubble and fell with a thump.

Hei's shoulders rose at the sound. The camel turned. Without a sound, Hei alighted from the tall beast.

"Running is ill-advised," Hei said.

"You saved *me*; you could surely help these people," Zun said into the grass. "I lost someone too, you know."

Shifu said, "Her father. Wang Fei."

Hei sucked in her cheeks. "Your father is Wang Fei?" She shot a glance at Shifu. "Wang Fei the machine inventor?"

Zun wagged her nose up and down.

"Well, daughter of Wang Fei, if you ask, I will tend to those people."

After Hei had given medicine to the old man and the wheezing girl, she invited Zun, Shifu and the boys to her barge. They all gathered at her dining table that night.

"Wang Zun, I have something to show you."

Hei reached into a pocket and took out some metal objects and glass vials filled with colored powders.

Zun thought she recognized some of them: red cinnabar, yellow sulfur, blue copper sulfate.

"Chemical reagents," she breathed.

"Yes. See these clever metal clamps, and this tiny spirit burner. Your father made them for me, fifteen years ago, and I still use them. Look at this," Hei said, holding up a thin rubber tube. "Do you know how hard it is to get one of these? But it's absolutely necessary for my pressurization work. I could not have gotten this equipment without Wang Fei. Did he teach you any chemistry?"

"A little bit."

"Aa. Your father," Hei said, "was no amateur." She was silent a moment. "So, Shifu, tell me," said Hei. "Why are you on the run?"

When Zun heard this, she cringed. She jumped in before Shifu could say anything.

"The Magistrate's men followed *me*," she said. "My mother is in the Magistrate's prison, and I went to Shifu for help."

"Why is your mother in the Magistrate's prison?" asked Hei.

"He thinks she is a rebel."

"Hrmm," mumbled Hei, shaking her head, and she cracked a black knuckle. "And is she?"

"She did nothing wrong!"

"I made a promise," said Shifu, holding his forehead. "I promised your parents that if anything happened to them, I would care for you. I would keep the children safe. What world do we have if the children don't grow up?"

"Shifu," said Han. He and Li looked at one another. "Shifu, we're old enough to go to the city and rescue Zun's mother. And we should overthrow the Magistrate. He burned our village and massacred our families!"

"Well, well," said Hei. "Sounds like the country is sick. In the body of society, the Magistrate is the kidney, and his unbalance throws everything off. But what can you do? Get rid of him, which is easy enough, and Beijing plants another in his place. The new one could be worse."

"The first thing is to rescue my Ma," said Zun. "I can go be a servant in the Magistrate's house – "

"Forbidden!" cried Shifu.

"Shifu, I have to get inside and learn the Magistrate's habits."

"You won't learn anything as a – what could you be – a kitchen slave? He has his own servants. You'll be far away from him. And you'll work with dirt, in filth, wet trash and dry dust – I can't allow it." Shifu paused. "Wang Zun, being a slave is a bad idea. Hard work is only part of it. Slaves receive no kindness. If they are sick or tired, they get no rest, no medicine, and they are beaten to work faster."

"How do you know it's so bad, Shifu? Did you ever know a slave?"

Hei looked up from her rubber tubing. "Shifu is correct about slaves."

"And that's not the worst of it," Shifu went on. "It's not safe for girls. The lords of the house – might not respect you." His words hung in the air like the smell of burnt garlic.

"Shifu is correct," said Hei into her spirit burner.

"Promise me you won't do it," Shifu said.

Zun's lips closed into a tight line. She could never make that promise. She knew what Shifu was talking about – hadn't she had enough leering chatter from Ba's customers? There must be ways to avoid attention. A big hat, or a bad smell. Did Shifu think she must always hide like a foot bound woman?

"I can protect her!" said Han. "I'll be a stable hand. They can't do anything without animals. I'll feed the horses!"

"As a new slave, you would not be the one *feeding* them," said Shifu darkly. "Stop this talk! You are children!"

"Well," began Hei slowly.

"Shifu, we'll be careful!" Han persisted. "You said yourself I passed the Invisible Squirrel! I can watch everyone in the house."

"Hm, well, and – " said Hei.

"You can't be everywhere at once, and when they lock Wang Zun in the cellar to give her a whipping, what will you do? And even more – there are traitors and spies among the slaves themselves. All day you must pretend you are a simple slave girl and slave boy and never reveal your name and never raise your eyes. Or other slaves will report you, or get jealous of you and spread rumors. You know nothing of these things!"

As Shifu went on, Hei silently heaved herself over to her camel. She returned with something wrapped in a white cloth.

"Shifu's right about the dangers facing a girl Zun's age," said Hei, unwrapping the cloth for all to see. Nestled in the folds was a small green silk purse, embroidered with rather chubby, wall-eyed dragonflies. "I made myself something like this when I was twelve. The one I had back then was not so pretty of course. I was a slave and had no silk. But every girl needs one." And she gave the purse to Zun.

"Say thank you to Hei Yisheng, Wang Zun. It is indeed very pretty," droned Shifu. "As I was saying – "

"Open it," said Hei. "Carefully," she added as Zun grabbed the purse.

Zun pulled the braided button loop over the big knotted button and saw several rows of small, upright glass bottles, some capped with wax, some stopped with cork. Threaded in the inner flap of the purse were two needles. The larger needle was hollow. Each bottle nestled in its own cloth pocket. Some bottles held powders, some, liquids. Shifu picked up a bottle of liquid.

"What is this? Soap? Can someone open it so I can smell it?"

"NO!" yelled Hei, grabbing back the bottle. "It's a sleeping potion. One drop will put a person to sleep for a few hours. Two drops, a full day. Three drops – forever."

Zun's eyes widened, and she pointed to the first bottle, half full of white crystals. "What is this one?"

"Inflames the stomach. Four grains."

"And this yellow powder?"

"Temporary blindness."

"What about this? It looks like milk."

"An uncomfortable awareness of the liver."

"*Wa*, can I really keep them?" said Zun.

Hei's eyes narrowed. "Well. Some technique is required."

Li and Han were all attention. They knew that giving out weapons was a personal and individual matter, and it would be presumptuous for them to ask for little poison kits of their own. Han could not help asking, "What are the needles for?"

"You use the hollow one to inject liquid. The other one, you can coat with a substance and prick the intended recipient. But not all of these are for ingesting. See, this greenish white powder is luminescent. Glows in the dark."

Zun was drawn to the bottle of clear blue fluid at the end. "What is this one?" she asked, holding it up to the lamplight.

"Oh, that one's very dangerous. A person who swallows a few drops feels deep contentment."

"That doesn't sound dangerous at all!"

"It's the worst. Because they don't know they've been poisoned, and they suddenly have no desire to move even a toe. They sit back and do nothing but enjoy the feeling."

"Is it opium?" Zun asked.

"Opium!" Hei's massive head rolled. "One-dimensional. Familiar. Predictable. And nauseating. No, it's a mix of my own. I spent years perfecting it."

"Enough distractions!" shouted Shifu. "This is all very fine. But a purse of poisons is not going to keep Wang Zun safe in the Magistrate's house. I forbid it!"

"Surely, a purse is not enough. She needs skills," said Hei.

"Hei Yisheng, Wang Zun's mother is my friend. She helped me raise these boys. A few weeks ago when she lost her husband, she also lost her right arm. I'm going to get her out of the dungeon. Will you come with me?"

"And what do you expect me to do?" Zun interrupted.

"You stay on Hei's barge, with the boys and Pig-Pig."

How dare he? This was *her* mother they were discussing! He was not her father. She came to him herself, and she could leave herself. He couldn't stop her.

"I'm coming too. And if you try to trap me here, I won't eat, I won't drink." She reached for something that Shifu might understand. "I won't brush my teeth!"

Hei snorted.

"Listen to yourself!" cried Shifu. "You're barely cured from that poison! Your mother would never forgive me if I let you get hurt!"

"Wang Zun, we'll go," said Li. "Think of the danger – and your complete lack of martial skills, and all the training Han and I have done over the years – "

"Shut your mouth!" she yelled. These bumpkin boys thought she was useless, did they? Must she prove herself to them? Well, they could fight. But fighting isn't everything.

"The Magistrate has a huge army," she said. "It won't be a matter of fighting the whole army to get my mother out. Please. I know the city. Ma is all I have – I have a responsibility. Don't you understand?"

"Shifu, let her," said Hei. "When I was her age – "

"When you were her age, you were an orphan, and you were so strong no one could touch you," said Shifu.

"Even so," Hei again spoke into her spirit burner, 'people had a habit of underestimating me."

"I go with you or I go myself," said Zun.

"ALL RIGHT!" Shifu bellowed. "We leave in two days. Wang Zun must recover from the poison. Spend tomorrow training – with Han and Li. Let's eat and go to sleep."

Zun felt a surge of happiness and checked the faces of Han and Li. Han looked smug, Li annoyed. "Li, I apologize, I spoke hastily," she said, bowing at him.

But he stalked away from her, pretending not to hear.

12. Danger In Saffron

It seemed as if her eyelids barely met before Han shook her awake for wu shu training at dawn. It was late the night before when they had finally gone to sleep after eating an enormous stew. Zun slid out of her bunk and tiptoed past the snoring Hei, out of the sleeping quarters of the barge and onto the marshy bank. Pig-Pig waited there.

"Follow Pig-Pig," said Han, and he turned yawning back to the barge.

"I thought *you* were in charge of my training!" said Zun.

"Yes. And I need to be well-rested for it," he said. She heard him step down into the bunks below the deck of the barge.

"How can a pig teach me wu shu? Don't just leave me here!"

Han's head popped up. "Pig-Pig plays every morning. He won't teach you, and he won't force you. Follow him and you'll learn."

Pig-Pig grunted softly and stretched his front trotters, leaning back on his rear. He slowly straightened his curly tail and let it spring back.

"And how am I supposed to do that?" muttered Zun.

Pig-Pig lifted his right front foot. He remained motionless until Zun lifted her right arm. Then he curved his back to the right, stretching. Zun did the same. He sprinted and jumped over a stump.

She followed him for an hour. They trotted over grass, zigzagged around rocks, leaned on their front elbows and kicked in the air, grunted and squealed. At the end of it, Zun felt wonderful, warm and light. The sun was now up. Han and Li strolled down the gangway of the barge, chewing rolls. On the bank, they each put out a hand and shouted, "Shi, zhi, jian!" Stone, paper, scissors. Li's face fell as Han's scissors beat his paper. Han smiled, tossed Zun a roll, and left.

Li said, "Eat quickly. Now we begin the real training. Stand like this."

They stood in a fighting stance, hands up to defend, knees slightly bent.

"Now kick with your right foot." He held out a hand to feel how hard she did it. "Again! Harder!"

She had no power.

"You move as if you're trying to cut bean curd without breaking it. Imagine kicking it to pieces!"

He made her kick over fifty times with one leg. Finally he let her move to the other. Then he showed her hand strikes: the tiger claw, the crane block, the panther fist. Sweat poured down her neck.

"Perhaps you should try a stance, no movement." He showed her the horse stance. He corrected her feet, her legs, her knees, her hands, her arms. And her face.

"Look straight ahead. Not too far or too close. Let your jaw drop. Relax the tongue on the roof of your mouth. Drop your shoulders – "

Know-it-all, mouthed Zun silently.

"What was that?" Li squinted at her.

Han burst out laughing behind him.

"All right, your turn. See if you can teach her anything!" Li stalked off.

Zun bounced out of the painful horse stance and rolled onto some grass, happy for a rest.

"What are you doing there? Get up, we're just getting started," said Han.

Training with Han was no different. She couldn't do anything right.

The three of them were silent at Hei's plentiful lunch of stir-fried vegetables, boiled nuts, steamed fish, and big bowls of rice.

"You're so quiet, you must've worked hard," said Shifu.

Zun nodded. The boys were expressionless.

"Well, you must begin your training – up here," said Shifu, tapping his head. "When you are out, observe the squirrel," he began. "It's a solitary animal. To the squirrel, any other creature is either a predator or a nut thief. The squirrel, therefore, becomes an expert at eluding capture and protecting its store of food. To do this, the squirrel employs a strategy some call sleight of hand, others call deceit. Either way, you must master the art of misdirection. Only go where the predator's eye has already been, but never where it is! Let the nut thief think it has seen you bury a nut." He looked sideways at Zun.

She wanted to giggle, but nodded seriously.

"We should spend the afternoon on the green purse. I have the contents written down," said Hei.

Zun happily spent the rest of the day in Hei's laboratory, going over the contents of the green purse. She kept the purse on her left, and practiced slipping her right hand under her jacket and pulling out the exact ingredient she wanted. Hei quizzed her on the contents, dosages, and indications of each vial.

"A number of these are deadly," said Zun. "What if I break one of the bottles accidentally?"

"I advise you to avoid that situation," replied Hei. "I blew the glass myself. It's thick enough. Just be careful."

So Hei could blow glass too. There were so many things she could do. Zun became curious about something. Maybe she could ask.

"Hei ..." She wasn't sure how to ask her question. "These are powerful weapons. Have you ever killed anyone?"

She sighed. "I avoid killing people. I lost my parents to fever when I was only six, so I never wanted to inflict that loss on anyone. But people have died at my hand – in combat. I used to treasure my skill at taking the one thing no one wants to lose – life – but a mindless fever can take it too, so easily! It is perversely unbalanced – " her voice deepened to a snarl, "something so precious is so easy to lose."

Zun understood. She had seen Ba's life disappear in a matter of minutes. She hadn't thought about the injustice, the ugly disproportion of it – two minutes of the assassin's work changed the lives of three people forever. She wanted to jump up and strike something.

Hei rambled on. "Maybe a fever is like a river running to the sea – inexorable, inevitable, though I doubt it's that simple – you can dam a river. But if you have a choice – well. Probably that Magistrate is a great nuisance. You might want to consider – if there's someone you want to kill – you might want to consider that by your hand or not, that person will be dead one day. Of course, if you must defend a life," Hei's eyes glittered, "soften no blow."

***

That night, Zun's whole body ached and burned from her grueling morning. She knew she needed to rest, but tomorrow was the big day. They'd leave for the city. She was too excited to sleep. It became late, and Hei was still not in the bed beside her.

Zun slithered from her cot and listened. Over the wash of the canal and the night breeze, she heard a murmur and followed it to the bow of the barge. Shifu and Hei were talking.

"How long has it been, roughly?" asked Hei.

"Few weeks," replied Shifu.

"Does the girl know they probably tortured her?"

"I don't think so. I hope not. *Aiya*, why did I let you talk me into letting her come along? It will pain her to see her mother."

"You heard her. She won't wait here."

"Well, my heart is sour. She should be studying or playing, not this."

"She's tough. Little green bean strung with steel."

"The boys can hold their own. They've had years of training."

"Wang Fei trained his daughter, didn't he?"

"He must have. She's a clever one. Still, she doesn't know what she's getting into."

"Aah," Hei sighed. "She has no idea."

Hei got up from the bow seat, leaving Shifu standing there with his hands over his sour heart. In the middle of the boat, Hei stopped. A night dove cooed and skittered over the shore. Maybe Hei would continue speaking with Shifu, and Zun paused to listen.

Instead, Hei snapped her face to the bank of the canal.

In the ghostly light of the gibbous moon, seven bald heads arose from the weeds. On the other bank rose seven more. Zun couldn't see their eyes, shaded under tattooed hairless brows, but the moon illuminated their smooth, softly rounded cheeks.

Hei disappeared inside the boat. There was a penetrating *poof* sound, and the barge was enveloped in haze. Zun felt Shifu brush past her in the darkness. She followed him down to the boys' bunks.

"Wang Zun – you are here. All of you, listen," Shifu whispered. "The malevolent abbess and her nuns have found me. We must change our plans! You three go with Pig-Pig to the city. Creep into the water. You must swim away. Hei and I will deal with the nuns, and join you later. Take only what you need, and be safe!"

Zun asked, "Shifu, will you be all right?"

Han jumped in, "Shifu, we'll fight with you!"

Li added, "They outnumber you seven to one – "

"Don't worry, don't worry. It's indeed disturbing to see serenity put to evil, but Hei and I will be fine. Follow me to the stern. Slide into the water. Make no splash!"

Zun stepped right behind him. She glanced behind her and saw Han and Li's agonized faces.

"I'll be all right," she hissed, scurrying after Shifu. She knew they'd want to stay with Shifu; that's what she would do. But she had to go to the city as soon as she could. Hei said Ma was probably being tortured – she must do everything in her power to save Ma. Including lowering herself into that black water. She refused to think about it and went right in.

It was all she could do not to scream. It was painfully cold. Her feet didn't reach the bottom of the canal and she flailed. A big watery disturbance by her side turned out to be Pig-Pig. Behind him were Han and Li! They came with her! The boys each took one of her arms and put it on Pig-Pig's neck. She understood, and held on as Pig-Pig swam ahead. She looked back at the barge, and just before it disappeared in Hei's smoke, she saw it tilt from side to side. Four rapid explosions burst in all directions around the boat – cover fire.

Pig-Pig, Zun and the boys came out of the canal about a hundred paces from the end of the smoke cloud. None of them dared to make a sound. Zun shivered bitterly in her cold clothes. Han and Li each linked an arm in hers, and she let them. The boys each had a sack, and Li carried his staff. She had nothing but the green purse.

13. The Price Of Pork

The sun rose and they dried off a little. As if by an unspoken signal, Zun, Han, and Li unlinked arms. The break of contact unleashed a flood of worries in Zun's mind: about the Magistrate's high stone walls; the big armored soldiers; whether Ma was strong enough to escape. Suddenly her plan of sneaking into the Magistrate's house, which she had thought quite ingenious, seemed ridiculous and full of holes.

Han stopped and looked at Li. "Stretching time," he said.

Zun went on a few steps before she realized they had halted.

Han slid his feet apart into the splits and lowered his stomach to the grass. Li did the same.

"Shouldn't we keep going?" Zun asked.

Han only leaned deeper into the grass and turned his ear to it as if he were listening.

They all heard a small crack, like a twig. The boys' eyes shot to Pig-Pig.

The pig widened his nostrils and narrowed his eyes. But he didn't turn towards any scent.

"I think it was a bird," whispered Li. "Let's go," he said in a normal voice.

"The city is to the south, not east," said Zun.

Li shook his head. "We might be followed."

"Shifu said not to tell her!" hissed Han.

"There's a ditch to the east," said Li, ignoring him. "It goes south, and gives us cover." And he started walking, the staff on his back swiping at the air.

Zun trotted after him, filled with dread. She had been so eager to reach Ma she forgot about the danger they left behind.

"Li, are you talking about those nuns? Who are they anyway?" The only nun Zun had met before was blind Yin Ayi from Chen village, who had been kind to her.

"The malevolent abbess, their leader, is a sister of one of the Empress's ministers," said Li. "Shifu said that the abbess gathers evil women to her temple: mercenaries, thieves and murderers. They chant and practice their own wu shu forms."

"With really awful names. Like Se Qi Fu – Death Seven Ways," Han interrupted.

"If they do not attain sufficient skills in two years, the abbess kills them. But if they reach the required level, they become nuns. In exchange for work for the minister, they get rich. They eat the finest fruits from golden dishes."

"Why would they hunt down Shifu?"

"Because Shifu and Hei took something precious from them, many years ago. We turn south here."

They had reached the ditch. Han and Pig-Pig swept in front of them, but found no sign of any nuns.

Zun tripped on a loose rock and fell, skinning her hands.

Li helped her up.

"You know, you really need to work on your wu shu. You move like a crane with its legs stuck in two bottles. Do you understand? Without training, you're like a lump of flour and water that will never ever become a noodle!"

"You're crazy. I don't want to become a noodle."

"I have soap beans. You should wash those hands." Li shook his head. "Those nuns could slice you to bits with their eyes closed."

Zun scrambled to the water at the bottom of the ditch, and scrubbed her dirty blood-streaked hands. The sun was halfway to noon. She shook the water from her hands, and ran back to the path. Li was probably right. She could be stronger. She needed to be her strongest for Ma.

"Hey, I didn't say to start running!" yelled Li.

Zun didn't answer. It wasn't up to him. They were finally headed south on a clear path, and Ma was only a day ahead. Pig-Pig caught up with her, and they ran on together.

***

At midday, Han dug a big radish from his sack and gave it to Zun. She scrubbed off the outer dirt, and bit away the skin. The juicy white flesh had a refreshing, sharp taste. She chewed it down to the stem and held out her hand for another.

"Aren't you going to eat the stem?"

She watched Han pick the grains of sand from the base of the stem from his radish, and eat it all up. She did the same, and pretended not to mind the grit in her teeth.

After a long afternoon's walk, with some diversions west, they found an old empty shack.

"We can spend the night here," said Li.

They sat down to eat roots again. Zun's jaws were tired of crunching. The sun set over a field of grey stubble. She turned to the south and thought she saw the glow of the city against a low cloud. Tomorrow they would be there.

"Why don't you take the first watch, Wang Zun," Han said. "It's the least likely time they'd attack."

Zun nodded. She'd have trouble falling asleep anyway. Even though she'd had no sleep the night before, she was excited by the thought of the city so near by.

The boys swept out spaces for themselves on the floor of the shack, and curled up around their sacks. They fell asleep in minutes – they hadn't slept much the previous night either. Pig-Pig lolled on his side with his ear flipped out at an angle. Zun stepped outside the shack and circled around it.

The waxing moon was already high in the sky. The only sounds were the swish of grass and an occasional coo from a night dove. She sat down at the entrance of the shack. She heard the boys and Pig-Pig breathing, and saw their dim outlines in the moonlight that filtered through cracks in the walls. Sitting beside them made her feel inexplicably safe. The worries that plagued her all day melted away and her head fell forward on her knees.

***

"Wang Zun! You didn't wake me!" Han shook her shoulder. It was dawn. They had all slept through the night.

Zun opened her sleep-crusted eyes. "I'm sorry," she gasped.

Pig-Pig grunted and rolled over.

"This is your fault," said Han to Li. "You told her about the nuns."

"*You* gave her the first watch!" snapped Li.

"Stop it!" Zun said and coughed, her throat dry as tinder.

Li chose a small turnip from his sack and offered it to her. She waved it away.

"It's my fault," she managed to say. "But we're all right. Can we just get going?"

Li shook his head. "We can't make a mistake like this again."

"We should get going. We've been here too long," said Han.

They filed south. Li broke away with Pig-Pig and searched the vicinity.

"Still no sign of any nuns," he said. "Maybe Shifu and Hei kept them busy for a long time."

"Uh. I hoped some of them would follow us," Han said.

Zun realized that the more nuns came after them, the fewer remained to attack Shifu.

"I'll take that turnip now," she said to Li. They walked along, munching.

"Han, I'm thinking," said Li. "I won't go into the Magistrate's stables with you."

"You worried about the nuns?" said Han.

"That, and what about when Wang Zun's mother escapes," said Li. "Shouldn't one of us stay out with Pig-Pig, and find a place for her to hide, or plan an escape from the city?"

Zun was surprised to hear this. She hadn't thought of it, and it made sense.

"You'll have to make some money," she said. "And find yourself a place to stay."

"Hmm." Li plunged into deep thought.

Han guffawed. "Li won't do it. Li wants to abolish money."

Abolish money! What kind of strange idea was that? Zun asked, "But how can you exchange labor and food without money?"

Han was still laughing. "He's just mad because we cleared a farmer's field one week, digging out stones and tree roots, and only got a few coins. Li said that was the end of it – no more money!"

"It isn't funny," Li fumed. "Who decides what a coin is worth? Who? And how do they decide? There are no rules! At one market the turnips are three pennies for a catty, at another market they're four."

"Maybe they had to work harder for the turnips at the second market," argued Zun.

"You know that's not how it works," he said. "Money is a tool of deceit."

"Well, even if you feel that way, now's not the time to abolish money. We can't go over there and start saying things like – "

"What kind of idiot do you think I am?"

"Look, have either of you ever been to a city before?"

Han and Li both shook their heads.

"We need to be part of the crowd. You're probably used to seeing farmers, but the city is full of all kinds of people: soldiers, merchants, scholars, and constables. The constables and the soldiers are looking for me. The Magistrate offered money to anyone who brings in the daughter of Wang Fei."

She paused. All that stood between her and the soldiers was a boy's hat and a floppy man's jacket. She surveyed the boys. *Oh no.*

"Your hair," she said. "You don't have legal hair. Boys are supposed to have the front of their heads shaved, and the rest of the hair in a long braid behind."

"No! I don't want to look like a Manchu monkey!" Li tossed his long glossy hair. Han giggled again.

"The punishment for an unshaved head is death. You can't risk it," she insisted.

"Are *you* going to shave your head?"

"No, I'm going to be a girl servant inside the house. I can't be a boy all the time."

"Then I'll be a girl," Li said.

"I'm definitely going to be a boy," said Han. "Oi, Li Jie Jie – Elder Sister – what are you going to do for money?"

"It's a lot easier to be a boy and make money," said Zun dubiously. The city streets were filled with boys working; she almost never saw a girl.

"Even though I'm twice as strong as most boys my age?" cried Li, picking up Han and slinging him over his shoulder.

"Wouldn't it be easier to shave your head?" pleaded Zun.

"Why don't *you* shave your head?" said Li.

Zun snorted. "Because it takes a long time to grow back, and – "

"Exactly! It's much easier to be a girl," said Li.
"You should put Han down now," said Zun.
"I'm not at all tired."
"Someone's coming."
Every time a farmer passed them, Han asked Li, "Jie Jie, what are you cooking for dinner tonight?"

Zun focused her eyes on the ground in front her, a hand on Pig-Pig's neck.

They stopped at a village to trade some work for pennies to get Han's head shaved, and a hairpin for Li. They went on down the main south road. Soon they saw the wall of the city ahead.

The guards at the North Gate looked very bored.

"We're bringing this pig to sell," Zun said clearly.

The guards just waved, and they were through.

They walked south to the center of town, passing many small shops, tearooms, and restaurants.

A dumpling vendor lifted the bamboo lid from his great boiling vat of broth. The warm steamy smell was a terrible assault on three stomachs that had churned through nothing but roots for two days.

"Do you have any money?" asked Zun.

Li searched his pockets.

"Oh, wait, no one can eat those dumplings," said Han. "That man's apron is like Pig-Pig's stomach when he rolls in mud. Filthy!"

Pig-Pig had many smells to investigate, and wandered off. When a few minutes had passed, Han stopped walking.

"Where's Pig-Pig? He should stay with us."

They turned back and looked for the pig. Down an alley, Zun caught a glimpse of two men struggling with a hooded black and white animal. "Pig-Pig!" she cried. She and the boys ran over.

"That's our pig," said Han. "Release him!"

"No, no, we are taking this pig to market. Get lost – *aiya*!" Pig-Pig kicked one man in the shin.

Han moved toward the men, but Zun pulled him back.

"Let me deal with this!"

Han glared at her.

"No fancy wu shu here," she whispered, and lunged past him.

"This pig is cursed," she told the men who still struggled to tie Pig-Pig's legs. She reached in and pulled off the hood. "I'm taking it to a shrine to sacrifice it. Look at its evil stare and wu shu exercises!" Pig-Pig lifted his right front and rear left trotters.

"The pig is pointing! Get out of the way!"

Han jumped aside. Li hung back.

Zun turned, and Pig-Pig turned, still lifting his front right and left rear trotters. "Whoever the pig points at – oh no, it's pointing at *her*!" Pig-Pig fully stretched out and pointed at Li. "She'll sicken and die, just like my whole village!"

The two men watched as Li began to shiver, then his eyes rolled up and collapsed, thrashing. Foam ran from his mouth. Pig-Pig stepped over to him, placed a front hock on his chest, lifted his snout to the sky, and uttered a long squeal so loud everyone on the block covered their ears. The two men were staring now.

Zun waved Han's sack of roots. "Come, cursed pig! Follow these roots!" commanded Zun. She walked without looking back, and Pig-Pig strutted alongside her, butting the sack of roots. Li stayed on the ground and groaned. Han ran over to him and helped him up. They limped after Zun.

As soon as they were out of sight, they broke into a run. When they were safe in the crowded marketplace, they finally stopped.

Han and Li both burst out laughing.

"Did you see them gawk at me on the ground?"

"Pig-Pig put his foot on you like a lion!"

"Wang Zun, that was great!"

She allowed herself a giggle, but their happiness was short-lived. Han gasped and pulled Zun and Li into a tent full of embroidered pillows. Pig-Pig ducked behind the tent.

"Look!" he whispered.

The marketplace was full of people, buying food, walking about. Zun didn't see anything alarming. She looked back and forth. Finally Han pointed and she followed the line of his finger. Three grey-cloaked figures stood in front of a roasted yam stand. In the late autumn chill, their feet were clad only in rope sandals. Along the hem of their cloaks peeked an under layer the color of saffron.

"Qi, Xi, and Ci are here!" Han whispered.

14. The One-sided Lock

"You going to buy a pillow, or not?" said the old woman in the tent. "You're just kids, get out of here!"

Zun bobbed up and bowed to the woman, out of sight of the nuns. "Of course, lady, thank you, your pillows are so pretty."

Han and Li sidled out and slipped behind the tent.

Zun followed. She whispered to the boys, "The Magistrate's house is just up the street."

"I'll distract them and lead them off," said Li.

"Watch out for Se Qi Fu," said Han.

They peeked around the tent to look for the nuns. They still stood at the roasted yam stand. Each of them munched a yam on a stick.

Li put a hand on Han's shoulder. "I'm going."

"Send me a message tonight. So I know you're all right."

Li nodded.

Zun's stomach dived. What if Han didn't get a message tonight? "What are you going to do? Don't let them see your face. Be careful!"

Li unclasped his hairpin and arranged his hair to cover his face. He ran off.

Han and Zun remained, standing still and watching. Zun hardly dared to breathe. The nuns chewed their yams and looked around the marketplace.

Li reached an open-air barbecued meat stand, which had a horizontal metal bar suspended on two posts. On the bar were hooks with cooked ducks, chickens and slabs of pork. Li hoisted himself up on the bar and stood on it at one end. People pointed, as for a brief instant he crouched, unmistakably, in the stance of the squirrel, thighs flexed, hands cupped around an invisible acorn. Then he jumped down and fled.

The nuns didn't miss it. Their cloaks rippled out in three different directions as they ran after him, trying to cut him off.

The nuns moved with terrible speed. Zun had already lost sight of Li, but didn't feel sure he would escape three pursuers. Pig-Pig galloped by like a black-and-white cannonball, and bowled the central nun down.

"We have to go *now*," hissed Han.

Zun followed him up the street to the Tribunal. She didn't let herself look back for Li.

Wide, shallow steps of black stone rose from the yellow-brown dust of the street. A gate of black painted wood bore huge carved characters, three feet high: Wan Zhou Fa Yuan – Wan Zhou Tribunal. Gowned scholars and armed soldiers were going in and out of the large building behind.

Zun and Han were the only young people in the small courtyard between the great gate and the Tribunal. "Look past the Tribunal," she said. "The Magistrate's offices and house must be there. And the jail." They could see a few buildings, not as tall as the imposing Tribunal but with similar curved tile roofs and columns of black stone, inside the compound.

"Let's walk around the outer wall," said Han.

Along the street, the wall continued for the length of several buildings. They could see peaked roofs beyond the wall. Around the first corner was a big gate where soldiers and horses came and went.

"The garrison," said Zun.

Around the next corner, the wall continued along a small alley. The walls of big neighboring houses lined the other side of the alley. There was one plain door along the Magistrate's wall. A group of dirty children played in front of it.

"This must be it," said Han. "The place you ask for work."

Some of the children were only half Zun's size, probably no more than six. Zun and Han were among the biggest. An older boy stopped.

"You looking for work too?" he spoke past broken teeth.

Han nodded.

"We got here first!" said the boy. He stood near the door. The rest of the children lined up behind him and pushed Zun and Han to the end.

All these children wanted work too! They were ragged and miserable. Zun wondered what would happen to them if they didn't get work. If Shifu were here he'd mend their dirty clothes and brush their teeth.

They all waited silently, but nothing happened. The door didn't budge.

Zun kept looking around, for grey-cloaked figures in rope sandals.

Han walked up to the door. "Let's just knock," he said over his shoulder to Zun.

The boy at the head of the line swatted at Han's cheek, but Han easily blocked him.

"No one takes us if we knock, idiot!"

Han looked at the boy in surprise, and returned to Zun at the end.

The children, one by one, got tired of waiting and drifted out of line.

Zun and Han just waited.

When their stomachs were gurgling for lunch, a houseman opened the door. The children scrambled to the doorway, elbowing Zun and Han.

"I need a strong worker for the kitchen," said the man. He stepped out and looked at them, hands on his waist. Han and Zun were clearly the biggest and healthiest, and he looked them over a few times. Then he shook his head.

"Too big, too old. You'd eat too much, and you're harder to train."

"But sir, we're good workers!" said Zun clearly.

"Then how come you're not working?" muttered the man.

"We just became orphans," Zun persisted.

"I only need one boy for the kitchen," the man said. He pointed to a little boy who broke into a grin of delight.

Zun just couldn't allow it. She reached into the side of her jacket and palmed a small bottle of blue liquid. Slipping out the glass stopper with her other hand, she lobbed a drop at the man's face.

It landed harmlessly on his cheek.

The man looked, irritated, at the cloudy sky above and rubbed his cheek with his hand. Then he tasted his finger. "Was that rain?" He stood there with a wondering expression, rolling his tongue around in his mouth.

The little boy he had chosen grabbed his arm. "Let's go inside, sir; I'm ready to work!"

The man looked at the boy as if he didn't recognize him. "Maybe it'll rain. That'd be nice. I'll just sit here and watch it come." He sat down on the ground.

The children stared. It worked – Hei's potion that gave complete contentment. Zun sat beside the man, and Han sat down too.

"Sir, wouldn't it be nice if we took you inside?" said Zun.

"You're such a pleasant child," said the man.

"Yes, and isn't that boy pleasant too?" Zun pointed at Han.

"No, he isn't. He's staring at me. I don't mind," said the man.

"Let me take you inside," said Zun.

"I like it right here," said the man.

"How about if we carry you? You won't have to do a thing, just enjoy the ride," said Zun.

"All right," said the man.

Zun and Han lifted him and carried him inside, seated on their arms like an emperor. Zun looked over her shoulder at the little boy and nodded him in too.

The other children started screaming and the little boy slammed the door shut behind them.

"Wouldn't it be great to see the kitchen?" asked Zun.

"I'm happy right here," said the man.

"Where is the kitchen?" asked Han.

The man waved a hand down the corridor. They made it to the kitchen, and set the man on his feet.

"I think I'll sit right here," the man said, sitting on the doorway.

"Oh, but it's wonderful at the stable! Where's the stable?" Zun slipped herself under the man's arm and struggled to lift him up.

"The stable's nice," said the man.

Zun and Han managed to get him on his feet. Han bent and lifted the man over his shoulder.

"Can you manage?" asked Zun.

"Lin! Is that you?" A husky woman emerged from the kitchen. Her body consisted of four parallel bulges encased in a white apron.

"Hu, how are you?" said the man, his head upside down.

Zun stepped forward. "Hu Laoban – Boss Hu, Lin Laoban must be carried to the stable. He hurt himself. I'm here to work in the kitchen."

Han scurried to the stables, lurching a little bit with the man on his shoulder. The little boy followed them.

Zun bowed to Hu. "I am called A-wai," she said. She took off her hat.

Hu looked her over. "I told that fool to get me a *boy*," She shook her head.

Zun bowed low. "I'll work very hard, Hu Laoban, you won't regret it!"

"We'll see."

The kitchen was enormous, steamy and warm. Weak white light filtered in from a few high windows, and oil lamps flickered from the rafters in the ceiling. In the middle of the room were chopping blocks and steamers. Pots and kettles boiled on a big stove. There were shelves of jars, sacks of grain, and baskets of vegetables. Cooks wearing cloth hats and dirty grey aprons chopped and fried and steamed. A pair of big girls prepared trays of tea.

Hu led Zun through to an adjoining courtyard, where a girl about Zun's age washed dishes in cold water. Hu didn't have to say a word. Zun picked up a flagon and started washing. *Easy*, she thought. She felt a surge of excitement. She was close to Ma! Maybe she could carry food from the kitchen to the prison.

After half an hour the work was not so easy. Her fingers were numb from the cold water. The girl beside her worked steadily and mechanically, never lifting her eyes to Zun's face. Servants brought more dishes to wash. Zun refilled buckets of water.

Hu came out and inspected their work. "Come now, in the kitchen. Time to wash vegetables. Bring clean water!"

"Yes, Hu Laoban," said Zun.

Zun lugged a full basin to the kitchen. The chopping noise was louder than before; the cooks were chopping meat. The other girl who washed dishes came in with a full basin. Zun smiled at her.

"I'm A-wai. What's your name?"

"Jung," muttered the girl. She had a pale triangular face, a tiny mouth pinched over grey teeth, and eyes like two dabs of mud.

She didn't seem interested in Zun at all. They washed cabbages and scrubbed lotus roots. Zun listened for stray words about the dungeon, where it was, what food they brought the prisoners.

"Ah!" Jung bent over and clutched her jaw. Her grey teeth seemed to hurt. Jung pulled a shaking little hand away from her face and picked up another lotus root.

Zun looked around. Everyone else was busy working; no one paid any attention to them. Hu Laoban was not even in the room. Zun walked to a shelf of spices and picked out whole cloves. Jung didn't bother to lift her head.

Zun tapped her shoulder.

"Here," she whispered to Jung. "Suck this on your sore teeth." She pressed the cloves into Jung's hand.

Jung scanned the room, terrified, and shook her head.

"It will help," Zun insisted, and pushed Jung's hand to her mouth.

Jung nipped a clove into her mouth and yanked her hand back from Zun. She went back to work.

Zun watched her make some timid little chews.

After the vegetables, they washed more dishes. When the sky became dark, Jung took Zun's hand and led her across the courtyard to the servant's table. Six servant girls were already there, serving themselves from big bowls of rice and salt cabbage. Jung picked up a small bowl and chopsticks, and Zun did as she did.

A big girl wearing enamel hairpins glared at Zun. "Who's she?"

Jung shrugged and filled her bowl.

Zun filled her bowl too. "I'm A-wai, a new servant."

"I'm not eating any less," growled the big girl. "Don't you be a pig." The big girl refilled her bowl.

Jung ate one bowl, and Zun decided to do the same.

Hu came to check on them. "I see you found the food. There's an empty bed in the room where Jung sleeps. Follow her there."

"Are you going right to bed now?" Zun asked Jung.

Jung nodded. She took a candle and started for the sleeping room.

Zun held her arm. "Please, I'd like to wash my face first."

Jung waited while Zun went to the courtyard where they had washed the flagons and rinsed her face, mouth and hands.

The sleeping room was in the south building of the compound.

"You can have that bed," said Jung, pointing to a corner cot beside hers. It had a thin cotton mattress and quilt. There were a total of eight cots in the room, in two rows of four. The room was cold. Jung took off her shoes and got right under her covers.

"How did you get those seeds?" she asked.

"Cloves," said Zun. "They help toothache. They have them in the kitchen."

"You mean you stole them? Very stupid! They flog hard for stealing here," said Jung.

"Huh! I know how to be careful," said Zun.

They crawled under their quilts and Jung blew out her candle. Even with her jacket on, it took time before Zun felt warm in bed. The other six girls who slept in the room trickled in.

Hu Laoban came to the door and waved a lantern over the beds. "Quiet now!" She closed the door and turned a key. There was the distinct click of a lock.

In the dark, Zun grinned. Not a problem for the daughter of Wang Fei. Ba had shown her how locks worked, and how to pick them. So she could do it; she had to do it. The needles in the green purse would probably work. As soon as the other girls fell asleep, she would sneak out to the prison. Zun couldn't wait.

There were muffled giggles from the other side of the room, and someone struck a flame and lit a candle. Two big girls carried the candle right to Zun's bed.

"Who's the new girl? What's your name?"

Zun sat up and blinked. "Good evening. I am A-wai. What are your names?"

The girls looked at each other and laughed.

"Oh, a little lady here!" said one. "Such a little lady. I'm Fan." She kicked the side of Zun's bed.

Zun got the message.

"The little lady has a nice jacket. Looks warm. Hand it over."

Zun looked to Jung for guidance, but Jung faced away from her, rolled tightly in her quilt.

She didn't see a way to keep the jacket. But the green purse was in the side pocket, and she couldn't lose that. She slowly moved her hands to untie the sash that bound her jacket.

"Don't take all night. I'm getting cold!" snapped Fan.

Zun pretended to rip her shoulders out quickly, and reached in to slip the green purse into the waistband of her pants. She pulled her arms from the sleeves with a big flourish and handed the jacket to Fan with a glare.

"Look at that face!"

Yes, look at my face. Don't look anywhere else.

Fan put the warm jacket on. She slapped Zun on the cheek. "Sash too, fool."

Zun's cheek stung and burned. No one had ever slapped her like that. Incredulous, she stared right into Fan's face. "What?"

Fan's cheeks mottled red in the flickering candlelight, and her eyes looked like black wells with little candle flames reflected in them. Even though Fan didn't move, she seemed to grow and puff with rage like a rooster.

Fan's minion grabbed the sash and yanked it off. Zun rolled on her side and curled up around the green purse. Someone kicked Zun's back, and she curled tighter.

They kicked Zun's bed again and went to their side of the room.

Zun took a deep breath without noise. At least the green purse was safe.

It seemed like forever before all seven of the other girls in the room fell asleep. Zun crept to the door and felt around the knob for the keyhole.

All she felt was flat cold metal. They'd put a plate over the keyhole. There was no finding Ma tonight. Zun was locked in until morning.

15. At the Tribunal

Zun opened her eyes and scowled. The morning air of the sleeping chamber was cold and stuffy. The lock turned, and the girls shuffled out for pre-breakfast chores. Fan snuggled into her jacket and yawned. Zun followed Jung to the kitchen, where they got water and fuel for breakfast. Zun shivered in her thin blue tunic. After the morning meals were made for the Magistrate's family, the servants sat down for hot soup. Zun savored every mouthful – but it cooled too quickly in the chilly morning air.

After breakfast, Hu led Zun out to the main courtyard between the living quarters and the official buildings. A huge roof and carved pillars marked the big Tribunal to the east, flanked by the offices of the Magistrate and the Chief Constable. On the west were the stables and garrison. Armed guards walked around a long, low building parallel to the south wall. Zun's heart beat faster. That must be the prison.

Hu cuffed the back of Zun's head. "Quit gawking." She handed Zun a broom. "Sweep all the walkways. Work fast. If you're not done before the scribes come to work, I'll get my stick."

Zun needed no urging to work quickly. Without her jacket, the cold was bitter. Even though she swept till her neck was covered with sweat, her hands became numb. Every minute, she glanced at the long prison building. Before she was done with the walkways, Jung came running to find her.

"Lady Lao told me to get a helper. Come quick!"

"But I'm not finished sweeping," Zun protested. She wanted to stay out and keep an eye on the prison.

"Are you crazy? It's all right with Hu. You'll work inside a heated room!"

Tempting. But Ma was just behind that wall. Zun kept sweeping.

Jung stamped her foot. "I didn't have to choose *you*! This is the Lady – we will be working for the Lady! Do you know how long I've waited?"

"You wait to work for the Lady?"

"Don't be such a woodhead! If you please the Lady, you can work inside! And do clean things, like make tea, and wear new clothes!"

Understanding dawned in Zun's head. Lady Lao was the Magistrate's Consort, the woman who had given Ma the poem about the lady with the heart of a hero. Maybe the Consort – Zun scarcely dared think – maybe the Consort would be an ally.

"Of course I'm coming, thank you, Jung!" Zun bowed in apology and followed her to the Consort's chambers. Long hallways led to a pretty courtyard, with glossy evergreen camellia bushes and trimmed trees.

"Lady Lao is most benevolent," said Jung. "She gives all the girls a turn to work for her. I've waited a month for my turn!"

"I'm extremely grateful, Jung," said Zun, who was thinking: *I better not miss anything that happens at the prison.*

"Is this where the Consort lives?"

"Over there are the Magistrate's chambers, and on this side, the Consort's," said Jung.

They passed through a circular dark-wood arch carved with many flowers, to a big room with a desk and many locked cabinets. The Consort sat with her back to them at the desk, and her personal servant, a raven-haired woman with wrinkled, heavily rouged cheeks, stood up and faced the girls.

"There you are Jung! Who's this?"

"Lady Ma Je, this is A-wai," said Jung, bowing. "She is strong. I brought her to help."

A disapproving glance lingered on the tattered hem of Zun's blue tunic.

"Follow me, then," said Ma Je, and they went into the adjoining room, Consort Lao's sleeping chamber. It was a warm, beautiful room, with a massive canopied bed, ivory inlaid screens, and dressers with mirrors on top. On the wall, above the Consort's polished desk, ticked a European pendulum clock. Zun recognized it. She tore her eyes away. Ba had tuned that very clock! It struck musical chimes every half-hour.

Zun tried to focus on what Ma Je was saying.

"Dust the tables, scrub the walls, mop the floor, and – "

Ma Je slapped Zun hard on the cheek. *Slapped for the second time in twelve hours!*

"Don't even think about the Consort's things," said Ma Je.

Zun's gaze had fallen on a pretty hair ornament, glittering with flecks of jade.

"*You* empty and clean the chamber pots," Ma Je continued.

Zun bowed deeply.

"See," Jung whispered when Ma Je left. "They're very hard on thieves here. Be more careful!"

Zun nodded. *Ee, for this I left the courtyard.* "Where do I go to empty the chamber pots?" she asked.

She lugged two big chamber pots to the big ordure jar in a back courtyard. As she poured the contents into the jar she could not help muttering, "Unutterable, putrid, nauseating filth – "

"What did you say?" said a manservant right behind her, with more chamber pots to empty.

"*Aiya*, stink, stink! Stinky! Sooo stinko!" Zun exclaimed, shaking her head and scooting away with the two big pots under her arms.

She really had to watch what she said. She washed the pots in plenty of water and scoured her hands. Shifu would be proud. She returned to the Consort's chambers and cleaned with great energy. The many candles, lamps and coal heaters had left traces of soot on the walls and ceiling. Jung and Zun climbed on stools and scrubbed them clean – a dirty, backbreaking job.

Ma Je inspected their work. "Quite passable," she said with a touch of surprise.

"It's time for the Tribunal," called Consort Lao.

Ma Je glared at Jung and Zun. "Carry the braziers and coal," she said. "And bring the fly swatters just in case."

The Tribunal! Zun flitted behind Jung, following her moves. Protecting their hands with cloths, they each carried an iron brazier filled with glowing chunks of coal. Jung pushed the fly swatters into Zun's armpit, and she clamped down on them. The braziers were very heavy, and reeked of coal fumes. Zun pointed her nose to the side to breathe.

Ma Je escorted the Consort ahead of them along the hall. The Consort had traditional lady's feet, bound to a tiny size, and she strode on them with deceptive ease. She wore exquisite handmade shoes, of midnight blue silk stitched with chrysanthemums.

The Consort had her own door to the Tribunal. She seated herself behind a carved wooden screen. Only the Magistrate and Chief Constable at the front of the Tribunal could see her clearly, but she could see through holes in the screen. Ma Je sat in a wooden chair beside the Consort, and Zun and Jung stood on each side of them. They arranged the braziers at the ladies' feet, and held fly swatters at the ready. Zun moved herself as close to the edge of the screen as she could. She could peep past it to the main Tribunal room.

Directly in front of the Magistrate's high desk was an empty floor space flanked by two constables. Behind this space were several rows of benches, separated by an aisle, where an assortment of people sat.

A stocky man and a boy of about sixteen walked to the very front bench. The boy was Hong, Zhang Ayi's son, who had helped her bury the Phoenix! His gait was almost unrecognizable. Instead of shuffling, he was brisk and straight. The short man who sat beside him was his uncle, Zhang Po, the newspaper editor. Hong was so different from Han and Li. His hands were tucked together in big silk sleeves. His hair was perfectly braided and hung in a thick shiny rope almost to the backs of his knees. He threw back his head to laugh at something Zhang Po said. He seemed so carefree. He'd go back to Zhang Ayi's tea and cakes, and he would know nothing of poison darts, and fighting nuns, and large women with scary nostrils.

Zun waved coal fumes away from the Consort with the fly swatter, and received a glowing smile.

The Chief Constable called out, "The first case before his Honor, Magistrate Jiang, is the matter of shop owner Di!"

A man walked up the aisle to the space in front of the Magistrate, bent down on his knees, and touched his forehead to the floor. He introduced himself as a jade-shop owner whose shop had been broken into the night before, and implored the Magistrate to investigate. The

Magistrate told the Chief Constable to take a detailed statement from the shop owner.

Next, two farmers knelt before the Magistrate for the reading of their father's will. The language of the will was ambiguous, and said that one son would have the southeast corner of the land, and the other son the northwest. The Magistrate nodded toward the scribes.

"You have the full account of the matter?"

One of the scribes said, "Yes, your Honor."

He told the two farmers he would have an answer for them the next day.

And so it went. For the next several cases the Magistrate made no decisions, but nodded to the scribes and said he would provide a ruling at some later time.

"The case of Kung Bo Lai and Xi Ni Gu – Nun Xi!"

At this Consort Lao flipped her fan closed, and Zun stared at the entrance to the Tribunal. A nun dressed in saffron walked in, rope sandals on her feet. She was one of the nuns Han had pointed out in the marketplace. She knelt before the Magistrate as all the others had done, but she did not seem the least bit cowed.

On the other side of the space before the Magistrate, a man and woman came and knelt. They moved as far from the nun as they could.

The Magistrate unrolled a scroll and read, "In the matter of the death of the boy Kung Bo Lai, in the Wanzhou marketplace, on the seventeenth day of the eleventh month: his death is determined to be an accident, in no way connected to the actions of Xi Ni Gu. The initial arrest of Xi Ni Gu is determined to be an error. Xi Ni Gu, please stand and accept this official Affidavit of Exoneration."

The kneeling man and woman lifted faces streaked with tears as the nun got up and took the scroll from the Magistrate. She tucked the scroll in her sash and walked out. Her gaze rested on the Consort's wooden screen. Zun ducked behind the lady's chair.

The man and woman slowly got up and left the Tribunal.

A fly came into the stuffy room, and Zun chased it. So she didn't see a prisoner from the dungeon enter, but she heard the shuffle of leg irons. A ragged woman with a stump for a right arm knelt before the Magistrate.

Ma! Zun nearly knelt. Ma was pale and thin, and her hair lank and dirty. But she was there, only a few yards away!

Hong and Zhang Po stopped what they were saying mid-sentence, and stared at Ma.

Zun glanced at Consort Lao to see if she recognized her. The Consort spread her big painted fan over the lower half of her face, and her eyes did not waver from Ma. The fly buzzed, Zun hastily smashed it on the wall behind her. The smack of her swatter seemed to have drawn everyone's attention. Zun bent to pick up the little black corpse and hide her face. The Consort gave her an irritated little look and resumed observing Ma.

The Magistrate removed his spectacles. "Chen Ru Lin, you are accused of organizing a rebellion against the Imperial Government. This Tribunal has gathered evidence of secret meetings, documents and plans. You have refused to comply with our requests for the names of your contacts. Do you have anything to say for yourself?"

"This humble person is Chen Ru Lin," began Ma, following protocol. "I am no rebel. I call upon Your Honor's faculty of reason to refute this so-called evidence. It consists of unverifiable rumor and innuendo. I am only a scribe, paid by the illiterate to write letters and documents. My complete records show every payment I have received for honest work. Your Honor can see that I have worked steadily for eleven years, and taken care of my family, and have had no time for government matters. I have no knowledge of or contact with rebels. I can offer no explanation for the accusations against me, for as far as I am aware, there is none. That is to say – " Ma made an effort, "your Honor's renowned wisdom can see through falsehoods concocted by conniving individuals. Your Honor can see that I am only a scribe and family woman, and the accusations against me are baseless." Ma lowered her forehead to the ground.

Zun stepped behind Lao, her knuckles white around the fly swatter.

The Magistrate put his spectacles on again, and read from a document.

"Chen Ru Lin, for your lack of cooperation, this Tribunal assigns you five lashes."

Zun shook her head.

The constables quickly pulled Ma to her feet and dragged her to a post. They picked up her arms to tie them around the post and realized that her right arm was too short. So they tied her neck to the post, exposing her back.

"Oh my. Please fan me, A-wai," murmured the Consort.

Zun saw Hong's face shocked and white. A constable picked up a braided-rope lash.

"The fan, A-wai," the Consort repeated. She covered her mouth and coughed as the constable raised the lash.

Zun opened the fan and heard the lash land on Ma's back. She couldn't do anything for Ma now, in front of the Magistrate and all those constables. She fanned the Consort in quick jerks and flinched at the sound of the second lash. Ma made no noise.

If Ma can bear it, I can too. Zun raised her eyes and watched them flog her mother three times more. As they took Ma from the room, Zun recognized the look on her face. Ma's mind was far away. *I'll get you out, Ma. I'll get you out tonight.*

16. Seeing Is Reading

"Oh these barbaric ceremonies," murmured the Consort, as they left the Tribunal. "How they consume my time."

Zun trudged after the Consort with the iron brazier, thoughts whizzing. *How do I get out of the sleeping quarters tonight? No one should discover that I am missing. How is the prison guarded? How do I get in touch with Han?*

"What's the matter with you? Put that thing down," said Jung. She had just put her coal brazier on the floor. "I'm thinking I didn't make a good choice after all. You'll get us in trouble, with your mind in the clouds."

Zun put the heavy brazier on the floor. She met Jung's glare with an apologetic smile.

"Wait for the Lady's orders!" Jung hissed.

The Consort flew to her desk like a storm from the south. The air crackled with her energy.

Ma Je turned to the girls. "Hurry up and get hot water – "

"Not now!" interrupted the Consort. "I need the transcripts. Have one of them go to the scribe room. If the transcripts aren't ready now I'll have heads!"

"Yes, Lady," Ma Je answered. "Jung, you go to the scribe room and get the day's transcripts. Tell them, *transcripts* – they'll know what that means. A-wai, bring hot water for tea. At once!"

Zun followed Jung out the door.

"What's the scribe room?" asked Zun. *Was it on the way to the prison?* She wondered.

But Jung didn't answer. She started to run, and Zun kept up with her. They passed big doors. Zun read the characters over them: Tribunal, Inner Entrance. Down the hall, a man with ink-stained fingers emerged from a room. He must be a scribe. He left the door open.

"The kitchen's that way!" hissed Jung.

"Right," said Zun, slowing down and peeking inside the scribe room. She realized she had already seen it from the main courtyard: a room beside the Tribunal and the Chief Constable's office.

Inside, there were four rows of desks, perhaps a dozen in all. An inky man sat at each one, busily writing. One of the men thought, sucked his brush, and dark liquid ran down his chin. He stared at the girls.

"Consort Lao wants transcripts," bawled Jung.

A chunky man with spectacles immediately got up and yelled at the other scribes.

"Finish up right now! Lady wants today's work!"

He gathered up the papers and placed them in an envelope, tying it carefully with string.

"Hurry back to the Lady, now!"

Jung ran back.

Zun darted towards the kitchen for the hot water. There was always a large kettle boiling for this purpose – tea for the Magistrate's family. As soon as Jung disappeared around a corner, Zun took a turn to the outer courtyard, where only that morning she had been sweeping, and ran west to the stables.

The back door of the stable led to its own courtyard, where men pumped buckets of water for the animals. She could smell horses' stalls. She chose a random aisle where men were working, shoveling out old straw and filling troughs with grain. No sign of Han. A few men lifted their heads to look at her. She decided to leave.

Just as she reached the door to the main courtyard, a shadow landed beside her.

"I've been waiting for you," said Han.

"Yes, but – "

"Li is safe. He and Pig-Pig led those three nuns out the West Gate, and doubled back."

"Oh, that's good news! But I saw my mother in the Tribunal. They whipped her. We must get her out!"

"Where are they keeping her?"

"I don't know. We must find the Magistrate's prison. I must get back to work, but I'll try to return this afternoon. See you then!"

Han nodded, and they separated.

"What took you so long?" demanded Ma Je when she returned with hot water.

"The kettle wasn't boiling," said Zun, panting. "Forgive me, but the Lady's tea must be hot." She bowed her head, bracing herself for another slap. But instead Ma Je had more tasks for her.

For the next several hours, she washed underthings, cleaned, and dusted.

The Consort and Ma Je were very busy with paperwork. They read through documents, wrote, and read again. When absorbed in reading, they paid no attention to the girls flitting back and forth with basins and dust cloths. Zun saw long sheets of figures, lists of supplies. It must be very complicated running such a huge house.

At one point while the Consort wrote a letter, Ma Je said, "Lady, the shipments of fruit for the Spring Festival will be delayed."

Spring Festival! The Chinese Lunar New Year. It would begin in a month and a half, the biggest festival of the year.

The Consort replied, still writing, "Send them a letter."

Ma Je took out paper, ink and brush. "I'm ready, Lady."

"Address it to Miao Ren De, Fourth District Canal Officer," said the Consort.

Zun watched and listened in awe. How thrilling – dictating an official letter! She wished that she could be the one to brush the letters for the Lady.

The Lady caught Zun's eye. "What's this one's name again?" she asked Ma Je, nodding at Zun. "This one looks familiar."

"A-wai," said Ma Je.

"She has a bit of light in her eyes," said the Consort.

"Impertinence!" snapped Ma Je.

"Oh, not at all," chuckled Lady Lao. "You see too darkly."

Zun bowed and blushed.

"Dear Ma Je is my protector and loyal partisan, you see," continued the Consort.

"Indeed I am, gracious Lady," Ma Je spoke almost gently.

"Before we finish our letter, give A-wai a needle and some thread. She should fix that tunic."

Under Ma Je's glare, Zun sewed the front hem of her tunic with glistening blue silk. The Consort dictated the rest of her letter to the Canal Officer. Sitting on a little stool at a distance with the needle and thread, Zun felt a familiar feeling wash over her. This was how it was when Ba and Ma chatted about work in the evening, and she practiced her calligraphy. If only the Consort knew that Zun, sitting right there, could write down everything she said as well as Ma Je!

As soon as the letter was done, Ma Je broke the spell. "Chamber pots," she said. "Empty and clean!"

Zun lugged them away. Now was her chance to meet Han.

It was late afternoon. In the large stable she had no idea where Han was. She started down the first aisle of stalls next to the wall. She heard a sound of repeated whooshing, as of a thin weapon whipping through the air. In the last stall next to a pile of hay, she found Han standing on the bare back of a huge brown horse, practicing a twirling figure-eight move with a pitchfork. When he saw her, he stopped and tapped the horse's mane.

The horse bent his front knees and lowered his neck and shoulder. Han slid lightly down and opened the gate of the horse's stall. "At last you came!"

"There's much to plan – " she said.

"Wait!" whispered Han. "Someone comes."

Zun melted into the corner of the stall and Han picked up his pitchfork. The horse ate hay unconcerned. It loomed before her, almost twice her height, immense glassy eyeballs, long yellow teeth. *It's a monster.* Even the fluffy tufts on the horse's ears moved with sinister purpose, twitching at her.

Avoid its gaze, she thought. It moved its enormous round rear away from her. Zun felt a surge of relief. Her hand brushed against the side of the horse near its stomach, and instead of flinching, it made a rippling sound. She held her breath. The wall of brown fur in front of her seemed benign. A thick maroon scar angled down from the horse's shoulder.

It looked like a strike from a weapon. She reached up and traced it with her fingers.

Li stepped into the stall.

"What are you doing here?" Han demanded.

"Change of plan," answered Li. "I got a job with the stable boss." He tossed his hair.

"I thought you were going to stay out in the city." Zun was confused.

"Yes, but, you-know-who followed us," said Li.

"The nuns?" Zun whispered.

"No! Shifu," Li whispered back. "He followed us here, of course, and he wants us to go back to the forest immediately," Li continued. "But we're not moving until we get your mother out."

"Oh no. Will Shifu be a nuisance?"

"Wang Zun, this is good news," said Han. "Shifu can take care of your mother when we rescue her. And then we can avenge our village. Listen, I've checked the prison, and it's small – only five cells, all in a row. I haven't seen your mother, but I know one prisoner is a woman. They feed them once a day. There are locks on all the doors, and guards."

"The locks aren't a problem. We need to deal with the guards, and find a way to take her out of the compound," said Zun.

"They put trash in a cart every morning, early, at one of the small gates. We could take her out in that," said Li.

"All right, that's what we'll do. How many guards around the prison?"

"Four. Two by the door, and two walk in circles around the building. The two at the door are the Chief Constable's men, and the two walkers are the General's men."

That sounded strange. Why two commanders, and two groups of men?

"I don't understand. Don't all the guards work for the Magistrate?"

"No. The Chief Constable has a small force of ten men. They have an office next to the Tribunal. The big army, about five hundred men, live in the garrison, which is that huge new two-story building, finished only a couple of years ago. Their commander is the General."

"What's the difference between the constables and the army?"

"The constables patrol the city and run the Tribunal. I've seen them bring drunken ruffians to the prison. I don't know what the army does. Small groups of up to twenty of them ride out of the city and back each day. I counted about three hundred horses."

Three hundred horses, five hundred men! "How will we get Ma past all those men?"

"Most will be asleep in the barracks. Some of the soldiers stay out overnight on patrol. We must be quiet and careful, and get rid of the prison guards. They get tea every few hours."

"Tea?" said Zun. An ideal way to slip them some medicine. She patted the green purse.

Han saw her do it and nodded.

They worked out the details. Zun was to meet Han an hour after the servants' sleeping chamber was locked.

She returned to the Consort's rooms with the chamber pots. By tomorrow, she'd be out of the Magistrate's house, and with Ma again! She could hardly believe it.

"Carry these papers over there," the Consort said to Jung.

The papers were clearly open for Jung to read. They made such a fuss when Zun looked at the jade pin, but they didn't seem to care if Jung could see the papers.

Zun approached the Consort's desk and bowed low.

"Lady requires more coal?" The brazier under the desk was almost out.

The Consort smiled. "Yes, thank you."

As Zun knelt to refill the brazier, she got a good view of Lady Lao's desk. In particular, she saw a thick document, lying open. It happened to be sprinkled with words such as "factory" and "tool-die systems" and "South American imports – " but that was not what gave her a shock. That was not what sent her hurtling back to the first time she had ever seen a brush limn a character. It was the form of the characters that locked her gaze, not the content. The document was written in Ba's exuberant script.

17. A Blabbermouth, A Buttonmouth

What was Ba's paper doing there? The document split Zun's mind like a fish under a cleaver. Maybe it was a clue to Ba's murder. Maybe the Consort could help her find out what Ba was doing until the time of his death. The Consort seemed to have a busy life apart from the Magistrate. Could Zun confide in her? There was no time to dwell on these questions. *If you fail tonight, they'll torture Ma again.*

That evening, Zun carried kitchen rags underneath her tunic. She went inside the sleeping chamber before the other girls and piled the rags beside her under the covers. As the seven other girls trickled in, she pretended to be asleep in her corner. Jung came in and disappeared under her covers. Zun waited as long as she dared, fluffed up the rags, and slipped out of the foot of the bed in the dim light. She crawled out the door and crept into the hallway. She waited around the corner from the sleeping chamber, and saw Hu Laoban walk to the door, swing the lantern around, and turn the key in the lock. She had them fooled – for now. It was up to chance whether Jung or Fan or some other girl would notice she was not there.

She had an hour to wait. Without her jacket, the cold was bitter, but she barely felt it. She decided to practice. She had only picked a lock with Ba once or twice. She found a padlocked gate and took out her needles, a few bamboo skewers from the kitchen, and some wire.

She and Han could not fail, at any point. It would mean death for all of them – her, Han and Ma. They had to succeed – in a few short hours it would be over, and she and Ma would be outside the horrible Magistrate's compound. What a relief that would be! Her hands were always chapped, her feet always cold. Fan was so mean, and Jung so weird. What must it be like, to sleep in that locked room, year after year? Never learning to read, day after day of boring chores. It must be awful, awful.

The needles were too short and too straight. The padlock was a big splitting-spring lock. She tried using wire, but it bent too easily. The bamboo skewers were too straight. So far, she had got nowhere. Everything depended on her ability to pick the locks. She wrapped slender wire around two skewers. She made a hooked tip on the end of one of them.

The big metal lock was cold, and her fingers numb. Her brain swirled with anxiety and the beating of her heart. She warmed her fingers in her armpits, breathed slowly, and tried again. She heard the click of the compressed spring.

Soon Ma would be out.

And what then? That dung beetle of a Magistrate would hunt them, and they'd have to hide – or run far away. Go to India or Tibet or Cambodia. Not north, she was sick of the cold.

At the thought of venturing thousands of miles from Wanzhou something metallic clanged in her mind. The Phoenix – Ba's bicycle buried outside of town. Water had probably trickled into the oilcloth and rusted the spokes. It would probably be immobile, helpless in the cold ground. It would never again wheel in the sun with Ba. If she left, it would never again wheel with anyone. She felt her stomach turn at the thought. This was no good – she was confusing herself.

Focus! But she had to admit one thing. As scary as the thought of rescuing Ma was – at least it was real; for the next few hours they had a plan, steps to follow. What scared her far more was the future, the immense emptiness of it. Where would they go and what would they do? Ma wasn't strong enough to take care of everything. Zun would have to plan for them. Where would they go? To the woods, like Shifu. A barge, like Hei. A distant jungle, in Burma. Well, why not South America? It made no difference. It didn't matter.

Before Ba died, there was a future. Ba took her to the foundry, he fixed clocks and telegraph machines and pumps, he gathered alloy samples, he chatted with engineers and cart drivers and the men who operated the canal locks, all for one thing – to build a bicycle factory. Here, in Wanzhou, where the streets were full of people pulling and pushing huge loads, going only as fast and as far as feet could carry them. What if, Ba had said, all those laborers had a bicycle?

What if she couldn't pick the lock?

She kept practicing on the padlock. She crept and checked for window lights; the Consort's chambers were still lit. Sitting inside that very room was Ba's document. Perhaps Ma knew about it. Ma could tell her.

Han quietly dropped beside her in the courtyard. Li followed.

"Do you have the things?" he asked.

"Mm," she nodded.

"Let's go."

She followed the boys to an outer courtyard. They edged along the building to the kitchen.

Zun slipped inside and waited behind some jars where she could see the cauldron of water that was always kept on the boil. A manservant poured water into a pot for the guards' tea. He lugged the pot out the door. Zun signaled to Han and he jumped on the manservant from above and behind.

Han covered the man's eyes and mouth, and whispered, "Quiet! Or you'll feel the steel of my knife."

Zun whisked the water from the servant, not letting him see her.

She took the vial of sleep medicine from the green purse, and put two drops on Han's finger. Han rubbed it on the manservant's mouth, quickly so he would not be bitten. In a minute or so the man was asleep. Han pulled off his jacket and hat, and put them on.

Zun counted out eight drops for the guards' tea. Han and Li dragged the sleeping man to the kitchen, and propped him on the wall near the cauldron.

The prison was in its own separate single-story building, near the office of the Chief Constable. Two constables armed with cudgels guarded the entrance. Two more soldiers circled outside the walls as Han, Li, and Zun peeked around the corner of the Tribunal. The front wall of the long prison building was windowless; on the short side wall, about the depth of a room, they could see a miserable little high-barred window.

Han put a finger to his lips, and then two fingers pointed to his eyes, and swept towards the guards. They would watch their movements first.

The two circling guards walked in opposite directions and passed one another at the short sides of the building. *Clever*, Zun thought. That way they could almost always see all around the dungeon.

Han took a deep breath, and emerged from the path to the kitchen carrying the tea. The two door constables filled a cup each and drank it. The walking soldiers were next. After giving each of them tea, Han scurried away.

The door guards chatted. The walking soldiers went their separate directions, slowed, teetered, and fell. Then fell one of the door guards who slumped forward before landing face down. The other door guard just stood and kept talking. Zun and the boys grimaced at each other. What if he sounded an alarm before falling asleep?

He however didn't seem to notice his fallen comrade. After a long minute, Han whispered, "I'm going to approach him from the side. You go in front and distract him. Pretend you're bringing him a message."

Zun nodded. She cautiously walked towards the door guard. He hadn't stopped talking.

"And you know I told him, forget about the peanuts! They won't grow here; they'll never grow here. This mushy ground is no good for roots; makes mush roots. Ha, get it, mushroots? I hate those things – the other things. Mushrooms."

Zun slowed down. He wasn't looking at her. He kept talking. She waved to get his attention.

"If you really want peanuts, I tell you where you have to go," he went on. "Gwangdong province, where – "

Han was almost beside him, raising a hand.

Zun shook her head. "He's asleep! He's talking in his sleep."

Han took the door guard's weapons away and together he and Zun lay him down beside his companion.

"Soak them in salt water first. Then roast them. They're perfect," the man sighed.

"Are you sure you used the sleeping potion, not a talking potion?" whispered Li.

Zun whipped a finger to her lips and shrugged. She didn't know, but it was time to work the doors. The front door of the prison had a crossbar and big rectangular padlock. This one was a little different from the one she'd practiced with. She poked her wire-wrapped skewers in and out.

Han squatted beside her and started to fidget. "Shall we take the weapons and hack the door?"

"Patience," she said. Now she was grateful for those hours of practicing in the cold courtyard. But this lock was stiff. *Please, let it not be rusted*. At a sudden click she gasped; it felt like a skewer had broken, but finally the lock gave. They were inside!

A single dark corridor extended to the left and right, lit by a few flickering oil lights. The cells were all in a row.

"Let's get out quickly," said Han. "It reeks!"

The odors of every possible kind of human excreta commingled in the air of the corridor. If terror had a smell, this was it.

Zun walked down to the first door. "Chen Ru Lin?" she called, careful to reveal as little of her voice as she could. Someone inside grunted.

"Chen Ru Lin?" she repeated.

"Shut up and let me sleep!"

Well, politeness didn't matter much to this prisoner. The next one was no better.

"Get lost!"

The boys had started at the other end of the prison, and fared worse. Li dodged a dark, noisome pellet a prisoner tossed through his cell window.

Zun and the boys met in the middle, at the third cell door.

"Chen Ru Lin?" she tried again, tapping the cell door gently.

"Ahh," came a high, weak moan. Ma! She could be delirious!

Zun kneeled on the floor to pick the door's padlock, trying not to be too distracted by the slime that seeped through to her knees. With shaking hands she picked at the lock, fumbled, bent her picks, and picked again. Han lit a candle and brought it over.

Click! It opened. They pushed the heavy door. A man ran out and bowled Zun over. Li and Han wheeled after him and pinned him to the floor. Zun shone the candle at his face and gasped.

Half of his head was lumpy and purple. His ear was a ragged stump. When he spoke only the good part of his mouth moved.

"Please, let me go," he said. "I'm on your side."

Zun went to the open cell. It was empty. He had fooled them. Ma wasn't there. For all they knew, he was a hardened criminal as well as a liar. Maybe even a murderer.

"I'll tell you what I know about Chen Ru Lin," he said. "You have to let me go! I'm one of you, a member of the Eight."

The boys and Zun looked at one another. The Eight? What was this man thinking?

"Let me stand up out of this filth at least," said the man.

Han and Li eased their hold enough to let him stand.

The man brushed himself off a bit. "I tell you I also belong to the Eight. I'm from Hing Long village, and you have to let me go."

"Hing Long? Is that the village next to Hing Feng village?" asked Han.

"Used to be," replied the man. "Until the Magistrate burned us down last year. That's what roasted my ear." He squinted at the three of them. "How do you know about Hing Feng village? It was destroyed years ago."

"Shut up!" yelled one of the drunks in the other cells.

"The Eight," said Zun. "Tell us – "

"Let me go and I'll tell you everything I know," the man hissed. "Not a word till we're out of here!"

The boys and Zun looked at one another. Zun gave a small nod, and the boys nodded back.

Zun grabbed the candle from Han, and put it near the man's cell. She shepherded everyone out the door. They hurried past the sleeping guards.

"And right next to that woman's lungs, where her heart should be, is a hard, round *onion*!" the talking guard said. "If you open it, you'll cry."

The scarred man froze.

"He's asleep," Zun whispered. "Let's go!"

"That's why I brought her those berries. No daughter of mine is going to grow a stinging onion in her chest instead of a heart. The family destiny can get on a boat and paddle straight down the river," the guard's voice echoed back at them.

Han let them to the garbage gate. Zun's heart pounded as they approached the outer wall. What if the prisoners left in the cells woke up the guards?

"This is the way out," Zun whispered. "Tell us where Chen Ru Lin is."

"You better not lie," said Han.

The man's mottled Adam's apple rose and fell as he swallowed. "I am Hing Long En," he said. "I don't know where Chen Ru Lin is. But they never brought her to this prison. They think she is a rebel, maybe the chief of the Eight!"

"The Eight? What's the Eight?" asked Zun.

"You aren't of the Eight? Who are you?" The man looked terrified, and his eyes darted for a path to flee.

Quick as two snakes, Li and Han grabbed his wrists.

"Oh please, oh please, have mercy," begged the man. "The Magistrate taxed us to death, and when we refused to labor in the mines for nothing, he burned our village! But I can tell you, to him I'm a grain of rice, and Chen Ru Lin is a prize pearl. Please let me live!"

Zun and the boys heard the desperation in his voice. But then they heard something worse.

"OI!" came a man's shout. "The prison guards are down!" A gong clanged somewhere.

Zun came to a decision. "Let's let him go. Ma's still here. We have to get back to our rooms *now*."

They opened the garbage gate with a creak. The boys still held the scarred man's arms.

"Wait," hissed Han. "Who destroyed Hing Feng village?"

"The Magistrate, of course!" said the scarred man.

Li and Han let the man go. He disappeared down the alley.

They closed the gate, waved at Zun, and silently ran to the stables. Zun returned to the servants' quarters.

She picked the lock to the sleeping chamber with ease. All was quiet at that end of the house, but she heard people running, doors slamming. She crept to her bed and her foot slid on a rag. She felt around under the covers – the rags were no longer in a neat, body shaped pile; some were on the floor. Silently, she swept up the fallen rags and pushed them between her mattress and bedframe. The other girls all seemed to be asleep. But someone knew she had been out.

18. Paths of Paper

Zun slept the thin sleep of anxiety, waking at the slightest sound. Finally she heard Hu slam her key into the keyhole as she did each morning. Zun sat upright. The key slipped and clattered on the floor.

"Hell take it!" cursed Hu.

Did she notice the door was unlocked? Zun trembled.

Hu flung open the door and counted them over. "All of you follow me. You're going to see His Honor." She looked grim.

Zun struggled to make her face a complete blank. *I did nothing last night, nothing.* She looked around, and all the other girls were the same – not a smile, not a frown, not a sound.

They filed into a large courtyard adjoining the Tribunal. The other servants were already there, on their knees. The Magistrate stood at one end of the courtyard, dressed in official robes. He argued with a compact man in constable's uniform, with a large black hat – the Chief Constable.

Zun bent down on her knees. Small bits of gravel dug in.

"I told you before, it was meaningless to retain him," said the Magistrate.

"But he escaped. That means his guilt is a certainty," replied the Chief Constable.

They must mean the scarred prisoner. Zun glanced at the other servants. They all fixed their eyes on the ground in front of them. Zun did the same.

"The prison locks were picked, your Honor. And a prisoner heard a woman's voice," said the Chief Constable.

The Magistrate looked fiercely at the assembled servants.

The Chief Constable bowed to him, and came to Zun's group of girls. He addressed Hu Laoban: "What did these girls do last night?"

"I locked them in their sleeping chamber, as usual," said Hu. "They had no way to get out and do mischief. I checked them last night, and they were all there this morning."

Zun stopped breathing. The rags in her bed had been scattered. Someone knew she had crept out – most likely Jung, who slept beside her. She willed herself not to sneak a glance at Jung.

The Chief Constable paced along the row of girls. "Any changes in staff recently?"

Hu pointed at Zun. "She started working here a couple of days ago."

"Hands behind your head." The Chief Constable looked at Zun's hands. From days of being on the road, and kitchen work, her hands were blistered and dirty, the nails ragged and black. "Tell the truth, urchin. Are you a rebel spy?"

Zun was so terrified she shook her head violently.

Hu stalked up to Zun with a long, thin stick. She whipped it fiercely on Zun's back, catching the spot where the poison dart had landed. Pain bit deeply into Zun's back ribs.

"Answer the Chief Constable!"

Zun bowed with her hands still clasped behind her head. "This lowly servant is only here to work, Chief Constable," she said.

"More like it," said Hu, and hit Zun with the stick again. The second blow caught her neck and right ear. The sting burned that half of her head.

The Chief Constable's eyes hadn't left Zun since Hu said she was new.

"New, ah. Teach her a lesson," he said.

Hu grabbed Zun's wrist and led her to the front of the group. The Magistrate slowly walked inside.

"Take note, all of you!" cried the Chief Constable. "This affront to the Magistrate's compound will not go unpunished. Those who helped the criminals escape will be caught and sentenced! And this new servant must learn her place!"

The chilly morning air seemed to magnify the crunch of Zun's footsteps over the gravel. Hu led her to a pole. Zun scanned the crowd. Han and Li! They were there, in the back. But the stable boss hadn't mentioned that *they* were new. They were lucky; the stable boss didn't pay much attention to detail. Zun limply allowed Hu to wrap her arms around the pole and tie her wrists together. Her back was exposed to the audience of hushed servants. She would just have to bear it. They had no proof that she had helped the man escape, but they were going to make an example of her. She turned her left side a little inward, to protect the green purse. If a glass vial broke she'd be in big trouble.

"Fetch me the knotted whip," said Hu to an older servant girl. The girl ran to an outer cupboard and brought a rope whip that ended in several knotted strands. A muted gasp of alarm rustled through the kneeling servants. Hu snapped a practice strike with the whip. Either because she was cold or because she was terrified, Zun began to shiver so violently her arms chafed against her bindings.

"Stop!" came the voice of the Consort.

No one had seen or heard the Consort emerge from the rear of the courtyard. Ma Je stomped behind her.

As soon as he saw the Consort, the Chief Constable bowed deeply.

"I'll take responsibility for this poor creature," said the Consort. "She worked hard for me all afternoon yesterday. All traitors and rebels will be caught and punished. This is just a child. Leave her to my care."

"My deepest respect for my Lady's charity and mercy," said the Chief Constable, bowing again.

The Consort inclined her head slightly at him. Hu untied Zun and pushed her in the Consort's direction.

Once again Zun found herself in the warm rooms of the busy Consort. After the horror of the morning Zun took a guilty pleasure in cleaning chamber pots and dusting furniture. Guilty, because doing those things wasn't helping her rescue Ma. Instead of Ma, the scarred prisoner was free. What had he said, about the Eight? What did that have to do with Ma?

"Please dust my desk," the Consort interrupted Zun's thoughts.

The desk! Ba's document had been there. Maybe there was a connection to everything that was happening. She cleaned all around the desk carefully but didn't see Ba's paper again.

A messenger called the Consort to a meeting about the Spring Festival.

"Go to Hu for your meal and some work," the Consort said to Zun. "If she treats you harshly, tell me. Oh, and wait." She nodded at

Ma Je, who shuffled to a cupboard and brought the Consort a folded garment.

"Wear this. It's plain, but it's warm." She handed Zun a grey cotton padded coat.

Zun walked with a light step across the cold main courtyard to the kitchen. She felt a small tap on her shoulder and looked up at heavy clouds. Must be a raindrop. She felt another, and then one more. No matter, for now she had an even better jacket than the one Fan had taken from her. She put her hands in her armpits and felt them loosen in the warmth. *I have to go out tonight*, she thought. *And check Ba's papers.* Maybe the Magistrate's house would be under heavier guard because of the prison break. She'd just have to be careful.

She left the sleeping chamber that evening without incident. The alley behind the garbage gate was dark, but a little rain had fallen and the air was cool and fresh. Zun felt light, with no one to watch her or order her around. She walked briskly down the alley toward the main square.

Her old street was deserted. The cloudy sky hid any moon there might have been that night. The familiar street laid a cold hand on her heart. This was where she had seen Ba crawl towards Ma in the moonlight as the horseman galloped away. She shut her eyes and pressed her hands against her head to still the images and sounds of that night. *This is just a street, stones, dirt and walls. This isn't my home. I don't have a home.* She'd slept a few nights on the cot in the servants' room, and before that in the countryside, and Hei's barge. The last place she felt comfortable in was the clean little bed in Shifu's cottage, now turned to ash. If she went inside, would the Fu building turn to ash too?

She had decided to tell Fu Gong Gong what she was doing. It was one thing to sneak around the Magistrate's house, but she wasn't going to sneak around the Fu family.

She knocked on the southwest gate and waited. She knocked again, just as she saw a yellow glow spill from the cracks in the door. Fu Gong Gong opened it, lantern in hand. He pulled her in, not saying a word.

She followed him across the courtyard to the north house. He closed the door behind her and whispered softly.

"Wang Zun, how are you?"

Zun bowed and whispered back. "Fu Gong Gong, I'm fine. How is the Fu family?"

Fu Gong Gong hesitated just a little. "We're fine. Tell me why you're here, Wang Zun. It's not safe for you to be in this city."

"I must look at my father's documents from the storeroom," she said.

He lifted his lantern to her face. "Must you?"

She nodded with force.

He put down the lantern and picked up a key and a candle. They left the north house and walked in darkness across the courtyard to the storeroom.

Once inside, Fu Gong Gong lit the candle. Together they moved the loom and the wheelbarrow aside and lifted the floorboards. The two boxes were heavy. Zun jumped down and pushed each box up, and Fu Gong Gong placed it on the floor.

"Fu Gong Gong," she whispered. "I need something to open them."

He nodded and passed her a chisel.

She opened the top box. It contained Ba's reference books – chemistry and metallurgy and mechanics. Nothing useful there.

In the second box there were orders of bolts, and designs for bicycles. She heard Fu Gong Gong shift his weight in his seat. And then she found a document bound with paper and red thread. *Transportation Study, Wanzhou Region*. That was it! That was the document she'd seen on the Consort's desk.

She waved the paper at Fu Gong Gong with a big grin. Together they closed the boxes again and put them below. She waved farewell to the old man.

"Wait," said Fu Gong Gong. He spoke softly. "Earlier, you asked how we were. They took my sons into the army. Both. Even the elder one. My daughter-in-law and the children miss him."

"Who took them?"

"The government, who else?"

Could this mean that the Fu sons were sleeping in the Magistrate's garrison this very minute? "Fu Gong Gong, do you know why the government is building up the army?"

He shook his head and blew out the candle.

Zun took her cue to leave. She picked up Ba's *Transportation Study* and followed Fu Gong Gong to the storeroom door. He walked her to the southwest gate, and locked it shut behind her.

Her next stop was the newspaper building. Ba had taken her there often, when he went to repair the printing press. Ba and the editor, Zhang Po, were friends. Zhang Po was Zhang Ayi's brother and Hong's uncle.

Zun cut through the marketplace, lowering her head so she wouldn't be recognized. The city's only newspaper building was in the middle of a block of newer buildings that didn't have gates and courtyards. Its two front windows were shuttered but outlined in light. Late into the night, people worked there setting type for the morning edition.

Zun had to swallow as she rapped on the door. Zhang Po's bespectacled face peeped out. He stared past her and Zun turned. A dark shadow slid away. Zun pretended not to notice.

"Zhang Susu – Uncle Zhang," she greeted him.

"Wang Zun, is that you?" he whispered. "Come in!"

Zhang Po was a short chunky man in a grey cotton tunic and quilted black jacket. He wore spectacles so thick his eyes were tiny watermelon seeds. He pointed to the document in Zun's hands. "What do you have there?"

"Not here, Zhang Susu," Zun said. They were on an open landing above the main pressroom, which was below street level.

"We had better go to my office," he said. "Come, come."

Walkways extended along the sides of the pressroom to the rear of the building, where Zhang Po and the reporters had offices. There was a strong smell of machine oil and warm ink. As Zun walked behind Zhang Po, she peered down at the hive of activity below.

About ten ink-smudged men prepared the plates for the morning printing. From huge trays of movable type, they hunted for characters and assembled them in columns in metal frames. The men were so busy they barely glanced at Zun. She heard one say, "Who's the kid?" And another replied, "Looks like a delivery for the boss." They kept their heads down. It took a long time to set the type.

Zun climbed a flight of stairs to Zhang Po's office. He closed the door behind them, and offered her a chair in front of his desk. She was relieved to sit. The office swam in newsprint. She looked all around at stacks of papers, papers tacked to the walls, papers on Zhang Po's desk.

"Have some tea. I was afraid you might be dead," he said. "I was sorry to hear about your mother's arrest." Then, unlike his sister Zhang Ayi, he looked at her and just waited.

"Zhang Susu, you know my mother was imprisoned unjustly," began Zun. "I have no idea why the Magistrate calls her a rebel. Or why my father was killed."

Zhang Po nodded and shook his head.

"This is one of my father's papers." She held up the *Transportation Study, Wanzhou Region*. "I saw a copy of this document in the Magistrate's house."

"How? How did you see the Magistrate's documents?" Zhang Po frowned at her. "When did you see it?"

Oh no! He was more interested in how she saw it than the document itself. "Zhang Susu, I wonder if you could help me understand – is there anything in here that could give us a clue about his murder?" She passed it to him.

He began to read. He was fast – he turned the pages quickly, but nodded and chuckled with understanding. "Your father was very thorough," he said, pausing at a page of diagrams. And then he came to a small chart of figures. The lamplight reflected on his glasses so that Zun couldn't see his eyes, but he stared at that page for a long time.

"Zhang Susu? What is it?" she finally asked.

"It's unfortunate he included this in his report, that's all."

"But why?" she looked at the chart. "This is just a listing of the taxes paid by a few merchants in the past three years."

"The Magistrate wouldn't want those numbers known. And it's … a little strange your father knew those numbers," said Zhang Po.

"How about if you print this chart in your newspaper? Tomorrow?"

"Never! Impossible!" Zhang Po tried to cover his consternation with a quick smile. "Have some of my sister's cookies."

Zhang Ayi's specialty, sesame-studded golden brown cookies that would melt in her mouth. She picked up one cookie and held it in her hand without biting it, thinking about how to make Zhang Po tell her more.

He began to fidget.

He burst out, "What's the matter? It's sesame!"

He was his sister's brother all right.

"Tell me the problem with Ba's chart," she said. "Was it bad enough for the Magistrate to kill him for it? Is that why he died? I have to know."

"Go ahead, take a bite!"

"Zhang Susu, I'm *not* hungry!"

His eyes narrowed. "Are you the real Wang Zun?"

"How about I eat a cookie, and you tell me about the chart?" Zun bit her cookie.

He put Ba's document on his desk. "All right. I'll tell you something about that chart. The Magistrate is not the only one who collects money from the people in this city."

"Who else? The Empress?"

"The Magistrate collects on behalf of the Empress. And there are other … groups. There's a branch of the Green Gang, for example. They bring opium into the city. They control a lot of carriers and barges. And gambling and other crimes."

The Green Gang! She had heard Ma and Ba talk about the Green Gang from Shanghai. She didn't know what it was, but Ma didn't like it. Ba's older brother, Wang Bofu, was involved in it somehow.

"But if the Green Gang controls crime, why doesn't the Magistrate just arrest them?" Zun asked.

"The Green Gang is too powerful," said Zhang Po. "They own banks and schools. This chart in your father's document – it's a big mistake. He never should have put it in there."

"Zhang Susu, maybe Ba knew what he was doing. Why don't you print this chart and see what happens?"

"Wang Zun, you're being like your father here; can't you see the risk? If I print this, and the Green Gang sees it, the Magistrate will be in trouble with the Green Gang and I'll be in trouble with the Magistrate."

"My mother is already in trouble with the Magistrate. If you can't help me, I'll deal with the Magistrate myself – before the Spring Festival!"

Even through the thick glass of his spectacles, Zhang Po could deliver a look that pierced. "What do you know about the Spring Festival?"

Zun paused. The Spring Festival. Of course, the Magistrate's household was busy with it. It was the Lunar New Year, the biggest festival of the year. Every day she saw preparations. Why was Zhang Po interested in it?

The pendulum clock on the wall chimed midnight. Zun smiled politely while the pendulum swayed, and thought about what she should say. She knew that in any game, you don't give up what you know for nothing. So she couldn't answer Zhang Po's question unless he gave her something. "It's late, Zhang Susu, and I must go." She gathered up the papers.

"You didn't tell me how you were able to see the Magistrate's papers," he said.

"Thank you for meeting me, Zhang Susu."

"Listen," Zhang Po said. "You want to understand what happened to your parents. I can't tell you. But I can give you a tip. Find out all you can about the Spring Festival. You'll find answers there. And whatever you find out, I'd like to know."

"Why are *you* so interested in the Spring Festival?" Zun asked.

"Will you do that or not?"

She nodded.

"All right, then." He tapped the *Transportation Study*. "Why don't you leave this with me?"

His shrunken eyes behind those spectacles gleamed. She nodded at him and handed him the document, when she remembered the things Fu Gong Gong had told her.

"Zhang Susu, I can tell you some things. The Magistrate is building a larger garrison. And recruiting many men into the army."

"Is he?"

"Do you know why?"

"The answer to your question," Zhang Po said slowly, "is in the Spring Festival."

19. The Promise Of Pork

The next morning Zun dragged herself out of bed. She washed two tubs of laundry before breakfast. Just as she sat down to some rice gruel, Han tapped her shoulder. Zun turned to look at him, but so did all the other girls. Without a word, she picked up her bowl and followed him out.

"I have much to tell you! But what are you doing here?" she asked.

"Your friend, the girl Jung. Bad toothache," he said.

Zun followed Han to the stable. Jung lay in some straw with her hand over her swollen face.

"She has a fever," Han said. "Shouldn't we tell the boss she needs some medicine?"

Jung shook her head and said, "No, no, no! Give me your seeds, the clove seeds."

He whispered to Zun, "Maybe the green purse then?"

"Jung, let me have a look," said Zun. "I'm going to open your mouth a little."

She touched Jung's swollen cheek and Jung winced. Zun very gently pried Jung's mouth open, and caught a glimpse of a yellow pillow of swollen gum with a black tooth in the center. She reached to touch it but Jung cried out and closed her mouth.

Tears welled from Jung's eyes.

Over her head, Han motioned pulling out a tooth, and Zun nodded.

"Get me water in a cup," Zun said to him. "Jung, I have some medicine for you. Better than the clove seeds."

Han returned with water and Zun put in a fraction of a drop of sleeping potion.

Jung drank it and soon became limp.

"Han, you're going to have to hold her mouth open." He nodded, and made a face like he was about to lose a tooth himself.

Zun pressed her lips together. How would she pull the tooth? She had some thread. She'd tie a loop and put it around the tooth to pull it, like Ba used to do with her baby teeth.

Jung's eyes were closed. Maybe she was asleep. But they fluttered open for a few seconds, long enough for Zun to look searchingly. *Will you be all right? Will you let me do this?* But Jung seemed to have no idea what was going on. Her face cradled in Han's hands, Jung looked completely helpless.

"Wait," said Han.

A long breath escaped Zun's mouth. She didn't realize she was holding it. "What now?"

"There'll be blood. Reach in my sleeve pocket," he said. "My last handkerchief from Shifu. I saved it."

Zun did so.

"Unfold it, don't touch the inner clean part, and rest it on my arm."

Zun nodded. She knew she'd never feel perfectly ready, so she just reached in with the thread. She looped the tooth easily, but Jung's eyes flew open. Zun pulled, and it didn't come. Jung made no sound, but her body stiffened.

"Hold her, Han," Zun said, and pulled again, harder. As Jung wailed, the tooth and its roots came out.

Han leaned her head forward, and blood and yellow pus dribbled out. "Put in the handkerchief," he said.

Zun rolled it up, clean side out, and pressed it into the bloody gap in Jung's mouth. Gently she closed Jung's jaws around it.

"You'll be all right now Jung, the tooth is out," she said. Jung's eyelids lowered.

"Pat her, pat her to sleep," Zun hissed to Han.

Soon she was deeply asleep, and they brought Jung from the stable to her cot in the sleeping chamber, with Han's rolled up handkerchief, clean inside part out, protruding from her mouth.

They were alone in the room, and Jung asleep.

"What were you going to tell me?" Han asked Zun.

She spoke in a whisper.

"I learned two things. One, my former landlord's sons are in the Magistrate's army."

"So?"

"So, you can find them and talk to them. Their names are Fu En and Fu Nien. Ask them what they're doing. But if you see them, don't tell them about me! They can't know I'm here."

"What's the second thing?"

"I talked with Zhang Po, the newspaper editor. He said we should find out about the Spring Festival."

"The Spring Festival? But that's all I hear about: the feast, the fireworks, the parade. I'm sick of it. What's that got to do with anything?"

"Zhang Po said it has something to do with my parents."

Han looked dubious.

"Maybe you can ask Fu En and Fu Nien about it. Tell Li too. When shall I check back with you?"

"Come by the stable after sunset."

"A-wai!" Came Hu's shout.

Zun jumped to go back to work.

"Go to the storage room in the southwest quadrant and fetch four tureens!"

Zun wended south and west towards the storage closet, always on the lookout for places Ma could be held, but saw nothing. The four tureens were wide and heavy. Holding them made her arms feel numb and sore at the same time. She popped into a sequestered courtyard, and saw a solid young woman with bound feet squatting with a bamboo pole on her shoulders. The pole curved with the weight of two kettle-sized stones suspended on each end. The young woman's face puckered in concentration.

"Shhhhh!" she exhaled, and pushed the iron bar above her head, opening her legs like scissors. Sweat dropped from her chin. She wore a thin cotton pantsuit that spread tight around her powerful neck and thick arms. Her calves bulged atop her tiny bound feet in sturdy rubber-bottomed shoes. She lowered the bamboo pole and placed it on a stand made of two upended iron forks. Beside the stand were neat rows of iron bars and stone weights.

She noticed Zun staring at her.

"What?" said the woman.

Zun bowed. "I am A-wai, a kitchen servant. I'm taking these tureens to the kitchen."

The woman pointed behind and to her right. "Over there."

"Thank you. Please, may I ask, where am I now? What is this courtyard? I want to know so I don't get lost again."

The woman picked up a small towel and dabbed her face. "This is my courtyard. I am Jiang Ming Wen."

Jiang Ming Wen! She must be the Magistrate's only child, his daughter by his first wife. Her only resemblance to her father was a small curved beak of a nose. Her thin black hair was pulled back in a hard little bun, exposing a round face. She sat down on a bench, holding an iron bar in one hand, and curled her arm toward her chest. She was so unlike any delicate young lady Zun had ever seen through the windows of a sedan chair. This young woman occupied the world like a watermelon in a soup pot.

"Thank you, Lady Jiang." By reflex Zun bowed, but the heavy ceramic tureens toppled.

In a flash, Ming Wen was in front of Zun and caught them.

Zun sank to her feet with only the lowest tureen clutched in her arms. She put her head to the ground in gratitude so fast her forehead banged the ground.

"My deepest sincerest thanks, Lady Jiang," said Zun, and meant every word.

"Hoh. Pitiful to be so weak," said Jiang Ming Wen in a generous tone.

For some reason the lady's directness put Zun at ease.

"Lady, you lift heavy stones as easily as the wind sweeps a cloud over a lake," she replied.

"Ah yes. And then my sweat falls like the rain. There's a poem in there somewhere. I'll ask my father. Go now, go now. I must continue."

At the mention of Jiang Ming Wen's father, the Magistrate, Zun became alert. She banged her forehead to the ground once more.

"Lady, may I ask, how can a humble servant become strong like you?"

"Oh, well, you can't. It's impossible. You lack training, a proper diet – there's no doubt you eat *noodles*. Worst and most irreparable of all – you lack proper form."

Jiang Ming Wen pointed to a framed collage on the far wall. "Bring that here."

Zun took the frame off its hook. Inside, under glass, suspended on red silk, was a fine specimen of a ginseng root.

Jiang Ming Wen took the frame in both hands and tapped the glass. "This is the ideal, you see," she said. "Look at its robust shape, the graceful tapering of its limbs. This is a worthy goal!"

Zun saw that, the lower part of the root was indeed forked in two and its upper cylinder had two protuberances. In short, it had the overall shape of a human body, with two arms and two legs. She had heard that the best ginseng roots resembled a body. But the converse – should the best body resemble a ginseng root? *Is this woman serious?*

"This is all you need to comprehend. This root is my model, and it should be yours."

"Yes, Lady." Zun bowed low.

"You're going to the kitchen? Fetch me guava juice and beef balls."

She trotted into the kitchen with the soup tureens. Before Hu Laoban could give her another order, she raised her hand. "Lady Ming Wen requires guava juice and beef balls, please."

The chef's famous beef balls were soft and delicate, made of hand-minced meat and seasonings.

Hu gave Zun six beef balls. Zun brought three to Jung.

"That's enough, please," said Jung.

"But you've only had two," protested Zun.

"I want to sleep now," said Jung. And she held the remaining beef ball in her fist, tucked under the covers. In minutes her breathing was deep and even.

For the first time since the tooth came out, Jung's face looked smooth and peaceful.

But that night, Zun was robbed of her rest again. Late, after everyone was asleep Zun woke from a kick to her bed.

Fan stood over her, carrying a candle. "What trouble you are," she said. "I should be getting my sleep."

Zun didn't answer. She heard Jung, snug under her own covers, roll away from her.

Fan hissed, "I'm going to tell Hu you were out the other night. I bet they'll want to know who's been sneaking around."

Zun thought, *if you knew before why didn't you tell already?* She said, "You won't tell. You're my elder and they'll hold you responsible. They'll blame you!"

Fan snarled, "Watch me," and stalked to the door. She lifted her arm and banged on it, shouting, "Hu!"

"Wait, wait! Stop!"

Fan paused. It seemed no one was coming. "What?"

"I'm prepared to make you an offer," whispered Zun.

Fan walked back with the candle. "Eh?"

Zun heard Jung murmur under her covers. "Beef ball."

"I can get you things," said Zun. "Guava juice. Beef balls. As much as you want."

"I don't want beef balls. I want pork buns. And if I don't get them by noon tomorrow you're dead."

20. Winter Baby, Spring Baby

Hu's apron-covered bulges loomed above Zun's head.

"A-wai, get up, up! You're going to the kitchen!"

I'll catch up on sleep when I get out of here, Zun thought, and crawled out of bed.

"And you, sluggard! Enough lying about! Up!" Hu kicked Jung's bed.

Pale little Jung reared up on her hands, blinking. Some of the swelling on her face had gone down, but she still looked uncomfortable and puffy.

Zun watched as Jung slid her legs out of bed. Hu watched too, eyes narrowed. When Zun made a move to help Jung, Jung shook her head and got up. Hu marched out.

As soon as Hu was out of sight, Zun took Jung's elbow. "Let's go together."

For the very first time, Jung gave her a grin.

Fan shoved them as she passed through the doorway, and bit at the air.

"How're you going to get the pork buns?" Jung whispered.

"Don't worry about it," Zun whispered back.

As they approached the kitchen, Jung pushed Zun's arm away. Hu sent Jung to the Consort's chambers.

Hu then waved Zun to a pyramid of cabbages waist high. "Wash these cabbages, separate the leaves, and trim them. These are for pickles, so remove all the spots!"

It was a nasty numbing task for a cold morning. Zun looked around at what the cooks were doing. There wasn't a pork bun in sight. The kitchen reeked of vinegar. Cleavers rattled as the cooks diced fish. The Magistrate's breakfast tray had preserved eggs with ginger, fish dumplings, stewed goose feet, and sautéed lily buds.

Someone gave Zun a bowl of rice gruel for her breakfast. She slurped it down and went back to washing cabbages.

Periodically she warmed her fingers in her armpits and listened for talk about the Spring Festival. So many distractions! Jung, and pork buns – but Zhang Susu had said that the Spring Festival held all the answers. She'd see if he was right.

When she finished washing the cabbages, Zun slipped from the kitchen, walked a distance away, and ran back. She arrived breathless.

"Lady Ming Wen requires a second breakfast," Zun told the cook.

Hu glared suspiciously at Zun and waddled across the kitchen towards her.

"Is that a dumpling?" cried Zun, as the cook spooned fish dumplings onto a plate. "Please, no, no. Lady Ming Wen wants only eggs and goose feet!"

"Oh, right," muttered the cook, 'give me that." The cook scooped the dumplings off.

Hu shook her head and shrugged.

"Oh, and more lily buds too," added Zun. The cook gave Zun a tray with four pickled eggs, a big bowl of goose feet, and a small dish of lily buds. Zun scurried out of the kitchen before Hu could count the eggs.

She wrapped two eggs, half the goose feet and all the lily buds in cabbage leaves, and brought them to Fan, who was polishing vases in a meeting hall.

"I said pork buns, idiot!"

"The cook said the pork isn't fresh today. If it's not good enough for His Honor's family, how could it be good enough for you?"

Fan popped an egg in her mouth with her fingers. She chomped down the rest. "Now – something sweet."

"Right away, Fan."

Zun still had to deliver the rest of the food. Ming Wen was exercising in her courtyard again.

"Lady Ming Wen, a mid-morning snack."

"I didn't ask for a snack."

Zun bowed.

"I apologize, Lady." Zun showed Ming Wen the eggs and goose feet. "The kitchen was concerned about the Lady's appetite on a winter morning."

"It's *almost* winter, not winter yet. Those look pretty good," said Ming Wen. She took the tray and ate everything on it.

Zun waited until she finished. "Honored Lady, the Spring Festival approaches," she began. "Is the Lady prepared? Is there any way this humble servant may help the Honored Lady?"

Ming Wen ran her tongue over a web of goose foot lodged in her front teeth. "The Spring Festival is a momentous evil. More noodles are consumed at that time of year than any other."

"Truly, Lady. A great affliction," agreed Zun. "Still, the Governor is coming for the feast of the fifth day. My father requested I read a poem."

The Governor was coming! That was certainly news.

"The Governor will surely anticipate with pleasure a reading from Lady Ming Wen."

"Hah! He and my father will have an insipid conversation about rebels."

"Rebels!" Zun looked left and right. "Where?"

Ming Wen leaned towards her. "That's why I think, instead of a dull poem, I should perform a feat of strength."

Zun clapped her hands. "Far more appropriate, Lady!" She wondered how to bring the conversation back to the rebels.

Ming Wen rested meaty fingertips on her chin. "Bring me brush and paper. I need some new equipment!"

Soon Zun was hurrying through the main courtyard to the farrier's forge, carrying Ming Wen's carefully brushed diagram of an iron stand.

The farrier wasn't happy to see her.

Zun gave him Ming Wen's diagram of a four-footed iron stand with a horizontal bar strong enough to hold her weight. She planned to do handstands on it.

"This has to be done *one week before the Spring Festival*," said Zun. "Lady Jiang Ming Wen requires it for practice. May I inform her it will be done?"

"You can inform her I'm a farrier, not a blacksmith, and I have two hundred horses to shoe, and armor to mend for a thousand men, *before* the Spring Festival. If she wants this done, tell her to go to a forge in town!"

Zun cringed at the man's angry yelling face with small gobs of spit flying out and cheeks wobbling behind black stubble. But the strong smell of forged metal was all around her, supporting her, lifting her like a ladder.

"I – I can do it, if you'll give me the iron and lend me a hammer," said Zun. "The Lady will be most grateful."

"A runt like you?" The farrier shook his head and loped to his forge.

Zun picked up a heavy ox hide bellows and squeezed a jet of air into the coals. The farrier looked over his shoulder and turned a piece of iron in the heat.

Zun pumped the bellows until the iron was white-hot. The farrier took it to the anvil and she handed him the hammer. Sweat ran down her forehead into her eyes, but she didn't blink.

"All right then, runt," the farrier said between hammer blows. "You help me here and I'll give you the iron."

Zun lost track of her burns that afternoon. But she ran back to Lady Ming Wen with the iron stand.

Back in the kitchen, Hu assigned Zun and Jung the task of cleaning the bird droppings on the Magistrate's favorite fountain. They each had a stiff brush and a bucket of water. Jung had some of her old energy back, but she was still quiet, and her mud-colored eyes blank as ever.

On the way to the fountain, Zun saw men unload heavy crates from an oxcart. Bits of straw straggled from cracks in the crates. What heavy thing needed to be packed in straw? Vases, maybe. Giant porcelain elephants or lions for some bloated decoration of the Magistrate's chambers. But as a couple of men lurched past her, legs straining with the weight, Zun smelled a familiar smell. Fresh nickel-plating. They held a crate of cast and plated metal parts! Sure enough, the characters on the sides of the crate said Pang's Foundry. Her heart bounded.

"Jung, this way," Zun nudged her.

"Eh? Fountain's over there," mumbled Jung.

"Come on, we need to see this," said Zun. Jung shrugged and shuffled along.

The girls followed the carriers to a far corner of the compound. There were no trees or other cover, so they had to stay well back as the carriers crossed an empty courtyard and stopped at a windowless stone building. There were shouts, and the carriers put down the crate and opened a trap door in the ground near the building. They loaded the crate into the opening and pushed it down. From below the ground came answering shouts: "Got it! Next one!"

The next set of carriers pushed the next crate down.

"Jung, what's in there?" Zun whispered.

"I don't know," Jung whispered back. "Is this what you do when you sneak around at night? Follow boxes?"

Zun didn't answer.

"We had better go to the fountain," Jung reminded her, and they withdrew.

As they scrubbed the fountain, Zun wondered about the windowless building. Could Ma be in there? But if they put machine parts in it, that would make it an unlikely place to have a prison. What were they doing with those parts?

Jung broke into her thoughts. "Soon it'll be the Magistrate's birthday," she said. "Maybe we'll get some cake."

"My birthday's coming too," said Zun. "When's your birthday?"

"New Year, like everybody else," said Jung.

"No, I meant your real birthday. I'm a winter baby. What season were you born in?"

"I don't know."

"Didn't your parents tell you?"

Jung gave a tiny shrug.

"How old are you, Jung?"

"Fourteen. I'll turn fifteen during the Spring Festival!"

Fourteen! Could Jung really be older than Zun? She was almost a head shorter, and so thin.

"How old are you, A-wai?"

"Thirteen," Zun lied.

"Oh, you're such a big girl. How did you grow so big?"

"Beef balls," said Zun seriously. "Ha, ha!"

Jung joined her laughter, and it seemed to Zun that that loud and happy sound skipped and bounced off the courtyard walls and up into the sky like swallows.

21. The Tiptoe Box

That night Jung helped Zun fluff up her bed with rags. She rolled over and went to sleep as Zun slipped out the sleeping chamber door before the other girls came in.

Again Zun waited for night to deepen before sneaking out the garbage gate. She passed through the marketplace on her way to the newspaper office.

Zhang Po seemed surprised to see her when she knocked on his door, but he let her in and led her back to his office.

"I see you have stories to tell," he said. "Let's hear them."

She told him about the Governor's planned visit on the fifth day of the Spring Festival, and the armor for a thousand soldiers. Interesting news had come from Li:

"Pang's foundry, in the northeastern part of town, has to produce five hundred guns two weeks before the Spring Festival. And they'll all go to the Magistrate's garrison. A shipment of cannons is late, but due to arrive any day now."

Zhang Po nodded his head. Then came Han's information from the Fu brothers.

"The Spring Festival is the code name for the Magistrate's big offensive. He's going to wipe out the Rebel Eight, a group of eight villages in the county. I don't know which villages they are."

"Interesting. And how does little Wang Zun know all this?"

She took a sip of tea.

"You'd make a good reporter. You already know not to reveal a source," said Zhang Po. "Well, I can fill in a little for you. The Rebel Eight villages are Chen, Hing Long, Liu, Wu, Lian, Huang, Zi, and Pao."

Chen village? Where Yin Ayi lives?

As if she'd spoken her thought, Zhang Po nodded. "Yes, Chen village, where your mother was born."

"We must warn them!" Zun exclaimed.

"But carefully. If the Magistrate learns they've been warned, all is lost. They'll just make a different plan. Leave it to me."

Zun ran back to the compound.

The next morning Jung shook her out of a dreamless slumber. "Hurry up, Hu's waiting," she hissed.

Zun flopped out of bed like a rag. She hadn't slept much the last few nights. She'd lain awake in her cot the night before, wondering if Zhang Po would get the word out to the villages, and what all of it could have to do with her parents. Well, they didn't tell her everything. Maybe they were involved with the rebels. *Am I a rebel?* She stared at her cot with disgust. A few months ago she only wanted a few things. Little things, like a seed-pearl hairpin. And some bigger, like a bicycle. She had had Ba and Ma at her side. And now everything boiled down to getting Ma out of the Magistrate's house, alive.

Hu broke into her thoughts. *She* seemed to have slept well. She thrust a mop and bucket at Zun.

"Go to his Honor's chambers. There's a mess."

Zun stumbled down the halls.

"Here, you! Clean this immediately!" At the threshold of a chamber leading off from the dining room, his old servant Fong waved at her. Behind him, an overturned chamber pot lay on its side in a puddle. The Magistrate stood some steps back from it, blinking.

Zun got to work.

"We'll replace this accursed vessel of unbalance at once, your Honor," said old Fong.

"I require clean robes too, Fong."

Zun bent her head and scrubbed the foul smelling liquid from the floor. She got up and bowed to Fong. "I must bring clean water," she said.

When she returned, she looked around, hoping for a glimpse of the Magistrate. He emerged from his rear chamber in a magnificent new robe, embroidered with cranes. He walked past her without a glance, into the dining room. Zun peeped past him. Consort Lao and Lady Ming Wen sat at the table.

Zun finished cleaning the floor and washed her hands with fresh water from the Magistrate's basin. No one paid attention to her. She padded into the dining room behind Ming Wen.

The Chief Constable was there too! She hid her face. He might remember she was the new maid. She bowed her head and pretended to wait on Ming Wen, sliding a dish of hard-boiled quail eggs closer to her. Ming Wen nodded in acknowledgment, and scooped four eggs onto a spoon.

At this the Consort smiled into her bowl of clear soup. Zun marveled that of everyone at the table, the Consort was the only one who seemed worthy of the riches that surrounded her. She had been the Magistrate's consort for fifteen years, the servants said, but was still radiant and beautiful. She must have been in her early teens when she entered the Magistrate's house.

Fifteen years ago the Magistrate was probably much the same as he was now, an absent-minded middle-aged man. Zun tried to imagine being just a few years older and walking into this house as the Magistrate's young wife. She didn't know how anyone could bear it. She'd ride off on the nearest bicycle, or even a horse, if she had to.

The Chief Constable put down his chopsticks. "Your Honor, about the number of constables assigned to me in the city," he began.

Zun slipped back to Ming Wen, out of the Chief Constable's gaze.

The Magistrate picked at a mushroom. "Did someone taste this? What's that about the constables?"

"I've seen an increase in disturbances of late. I'd like to add three more men to my force."

"So do it. You manage your own force. What do I care?"

The Consort snapped out her fan and watched the two men.

"But, your Honor, last time I made this request by letter you clearly stated that the budget would not allow – "

"Well, if I already replied, you must accept your answer."

"Times have changed, your Honor – "

"Indeed they have. But the last noticeable change in this miserable backwater was a thousand years ago. The Song Dynasty – now they could run a country. Fong – paper and brushes! Hurry!"

Zun watched Consort Lao with pity. What a family to be mired in. A husband stuck in the Song Dynasty, and his daughter, the ginseng root. How the Consort must have suffered all these years. It was like Ma said: the wife must carry the weight of the husband's troubles – or habits – like a four-hundred-pound coat. The Lady caught Zun's eye. Zun smiled warmly back at her and bowed low.

The Magistrate brushed lightly and quickly on his paper.

Zun pushed more meatballs at Ming Wen.

"I am finished," said the Magistrate. "Hear this!"

And he read from his freshly brushed paper:

Dear Little Lao,
Moments of camellias, years of mountains,
And you my precious nightjar. Your mountain song
Falls in camellia moments to my ears.

Was this a poem?

"What do you think, Chief Constable?" the Magistrate asked.

"I am speechless, your Honor," said the Chief Constable. "I could not dream of ascending to your level of literacy."

The Chief Constable waved the newspaper.

"I think you need to see this, your Honor," he said.

The Consort looked up, and the Magistrate adjusted his robe so that it flowed smoothly over his chair.

"News from Beijing?" the Magistrate asked.

"No, your Honor, the newspaper has a series of articles written by … your Honor."

"It's too soon after my poem for jest and banter," said the Magistrate.

"Unfortunately, your Honor, I do not jest. There is a series of articles here about the canal system. The newspaper quotes your official documents, word for word."

What did Zhang Po do? Did he quote only from the Magistrate's own documents? How clever he is, Zun thought.

"In a newspaper read by common people? Unthinkable!" The Magistrate seized the paper and scanned it. "What is this – '*in response to Canal Engineer Shen's report on the need for canal drainage*'

– hopeless bore, canal drainage – '*the Magistrate rules that insufficient funds are available this year for canal repair*' – I should think so! Look at this – '*Building of the Pavilions at Tiger Hill Gardens will commence in the spring*' – well, the explanation is simple. Lies! Pure lies!"

The Chief Constable smiled. And kept smiling. "Yes, your Honor, but I think these articles convey – perhaps not the truth exactly – but –"

"I know these are all lies, because I didn't write these words. Not one!"

"Your Honor can't be expected to memorize all of the – "

"I tell you I didn't write a word of this! The style is quite good – superior to the norm. Not as good as mine of course."

"Please let me see," the Consort said.

The Magistrate handed it to her and rose. "This meal is done," he said. "Fong, get me my official robe."

Zun was about to slip out and follow him when the Consort addressed her.

"Little maid. A-wai, is it? I have tasks for you. Follow us."

Ma Je came to the table and helped the Consort stand. They walked to the Consort's chambers and Zun followed. They went back through the beautiful carved wooden arch to the Consort's warm room. The European clock on the wall chimed nine o'clock.

For the next two hours Zun dusted the Consort's pretty ornaments and carried messages about the Spring Festival feast preparations to and from the kitchen. The Magistrate kept the Consort busy with the management of his house, to hide his real motive of massacring eight villages. Zun's heart burned. Maybe a moment would come when she could tell the Consort what was really going on.

A little past eleven o'clock a manservant came to the Consort's chamber. Before he could even open his mouth the Consort said, "A-wai, please report to Hu in the kitchen. Thank you for your work this morning."

Zun was free! Hu wouldn't know exactly when the Consort dismissed her. She bowed to the Consort and all but skipped out. She had maybe a precious hour to wander the compound. Hu would expect her for lunch.

But maybe she should do something different. Maybe she should find a way to speak to the Consort. Somewhere in the compound Ma was hidden. The Consort might know a way to find her. Zun stopped on a courtyard bench to think.

Ma Je and the Consort emerged, and Zun sprang behind a trellis. They passed by, near enough for Zun to hear the Consort speaking.

"This is how it goes. He promised to help, and now look. Zhang Po is a rebel mouthpiece."

Zhang Po? The newspaper editor?

"I ordered them to put him in the Tiptoe box in the morning. By tomorrow night he'll be dead." She chuckled. "So the Spring Festival begins a little early."

22. The Lady Under The Osmanthus

Zun felt as if a knife was being twisted in her stomach. Zhang Po in the Tiptoe box! That dreadful device she and the boys had seen the day they walked into the city. The condemned man was tied into the box and had to stand on tiptoe to stay alive. She had to warn Zhang Po! Forgetting the consequences, she tore through the compound and out the main gate.

Rage sped her feet. She didn't know what was worse. That it was Zhang Po. That it was the Tiptoe box. Or that it was the Consort who ordered it, the Consort who Zun had so admired. *I can't believe I cleaned her chamber pots. As well as I could.*

She ran through the streets, not caring if anyone recognized her. But when she reached the newspaper building, she was too late. The soldiers had reached Zhang Po before her. They locked his legs in irons and put him on a cart. He lowered his face in shame.

She followed them back to the compound and saw them lock him in the prison.

"He's going in the Tiptoe in the morning," she heard a guard say. So it was confirmed. Zun stood in the main courtyard and twisted the hem of her jacket in her hands.

"A-wai! What are you doing here? Go to the kitchen and scrub roots!" Hu cried.

Zun trotted back. She scraped and cleaned lotus roots as her mind churned. Jung came to get her for lunch.

"That looks like far too many roots," she said. "Will you come with me to the Consort's chambers this afternoon?"

"Mm!" Zun grunted.

Her face was so tense that Jung asked, "What's the matter? Toothache?"

That afternoon Zun watched the Consort's every move. She sat at her desk for a solid hour. Ma Je sat near her. Ma Je worked on household accounts. The Consort wrote letters, and frequently used the carved golden jade seals on her desk. She had a special pad of red ink for the seals. There was nothing unusual about that. At the end of the hour the Consort stretched her arms. Her wide silk sleeves rippled, revealing embroidered peonies. She looked at Jung and Zun polishing a carved screen.

"Ma Je, please give the girls a cake each," she said.

Zun bowed deeply under Ma Je's glare. The cake was almond, and delicious. Zun crunched it down. The afternoon continued like that, with the Consort busy working, enjoying herself, and Zun feeling like a caged tiger. She had to do something for Zhang Po, but she didn't know what. Later in the afternoon she escaped to the stable and found Han.

"I have things to tell *you*," Han said, as soon as he saw her, and led them to the stall of the big brown horse.

Before he could speak a word, she said, "Han, I discovered something horrible."

"What, is your mother all right?"

"I don't know. But remember that nasty box we saw when we came to the city, with the dying man in it? The Tiptoe box?"

Han nodded.

"The Consort ordered Zhang Po to be put in it tomorrow morning!"

"Really?" Han said. "Is he being kept in the prison? Should we get him out tonight?"

"Of course we should!"

"But it won't be easy. Ever since the other prison break they've doubled the guards." He paused, and then said, "Before I forget, let me tell you what I've seen. I've been watching Magistrate Jiang. He's the laziest man alive. He gets up, writes a few characters – not even a whole poem, eats, drinks tea, sits and thinks, and that's it. This morning, for example – someone told him Engineer Shen was in that courtyard. They gave him a scroll to read, and he read it. Then he went back to his chambers and took a bath. The Chief Constable went to Engineer Shen."

"Thinking is working," Zun said.

"He doesn't think about anything to do with his work. I climbed into his ceiling and watched him write. He brushes a lot of nothing. Clouds and birds and frogs."

She couldn't believe he was so idle, not after she witnessed the constant, concentrated activity in the Consort's chambers. Once again she remembered the golden jade seals.

"So you've never seen him brush and stamp a document with his official seal?" Zun asked.

"No, never."

"Well, all those scrolls in the scribe room didn't write themselves." Suddenly she recalled the scene at the breakfast table the day before. "When the Magistrate read the newspaper yesterday, he claimed it was all lies. He said he didn't write a word of it! I was sure he was lying. But maybe he wasn't."

She stopped breathing. What if –

"What is it, Wang Zun? You look like Li after he gets a haircut."

"Lady Lao – the Consort – she has some very fancy seals."

Zun felt her mouth get so dry her cheeks stuck to her teeth. She swallowed. "The Consort and her servant Ma Je are *always* working. They read documents, they write them. They send things back and forth from the scribe room. They plan every detail of the Spring Festival!"

A terrible suspicion formed in her mind. She had to find proof. If it was true, then she knew what she had to do.

"Han, I need your help. We have to get into the Consort's chambers and the scribe room!"

***

That night, Zun ground osmanthus petals with her teeth to a smooth paste, and swallowed them.

She dipped her hands into the icy basin again. Good that her fingers were numb and could hardly feel the cold water. The insides of her hands rang with a dull pain. She hoped it wouldn't get worse; she could stand no more. She dried her hands and dusted them with white flour. She surveyed her face in the polished tin pan she had brought from the kitchen. Her cheeks were a pale, greenish white. Her lower eyelids were coated with charcoal. Purple and green shadows traced her temples. Her hair, stiffened with cold white grease, hung in lank ropes around her face. Her body was loosely draped in a white wide-sleeved tunic of Ming Wen's that she'd stolen from the laundry.

She crept along the hallway to the Magistrate's sleeping chamber, waiting for Old Fong's exit. Finally, she heard the tottering beat of his footsteps, and peeked in at the door. An aroma of freshly brewed tea floated from the Magistrate's room.

The old man sat at his desk, bent over paper, his brush in hand. He chewed the end of the brush. He pointed and flexed his feet. He murmured, "Old thrush … flower … purple … Is it purple or red?"

Zun crept up behind him and listened. The Magistrate started again.

"Old thrush flowers a purple song," he chanted.

Zun silently skittered around the room and flapped her sleeves over each lamp. The flames flickered and went out, and the Magistrate's head popped up. In the dimness, she wafted over to the Magistrate and folded her cold hands around his right hand, the one holding his brush.

The Magistrate could not speak for gasping.

"Your Honor. Your Honor, look at me." Zun released her hands, which were starting to warm up, and spoke to the Magistrate. A glint of moonlight from the window was enough to hint at her ghostly face. "I come from under the osmanthus tree," she began.

"The Lady Under the Osmanthus," the Magistrate whispered. "I … I don't remember any lady under – "

"Wu Chen Bo buried me under the osmanthus tree a century ago, and I awake with the winds of Hell."

The Magistrate's jaw hung loose with terror.

"But why come to me, Lady?"

"I cannot rest, for I was denied my place at court," said Zun, as menacingly as she could. "Where are your Tribunal documents?"

"They … they are in the scribe room, Lady, though the underworld takes interest in bureaucracy, I cannot – "

"I come because of your daughter, Jiang Ming Wen. You have failed her!"

"Ming Wen? But everything is arranged for Ming Wen! I have arranged for a dowry as big as a city treasury. She has beautiful silks and jewels. I even found her a husband, Shen Hong, the engineer's son."

"A*iarrrrrrrrrruhhhh*," Zun turned a shocked *aiya* to a ghostly groan of distaste. Hong to marry the ginseng root? She raised a threateningly long sleeve. "You forget the most important of preparations! You have done nothing!"

"What? What can you mean?"

"A woman who puts three whole chicken eggs in her mouth at once will never command respect in society!"

The Magistrate no doubt recalled his daughter at their last meal together, her cheeks full of meatballs.

"I will repair my hideous neglect immediately!" he said. "I will send her to Shanghai – "

"Do as I say! You must send Consort Lao to instruct her!"

"Lady Lao! But she is most preoccupied with the Spring Festival; she has not a minute to spare – "

"Is any woman in Shanghai more cultivated than Consort Lao? More delicate? More complete in feminine wisdom?"

The Magistrate shook his head. "Impossible, impossible."

"Have the Consort begin Ming Wen's training immediately! Or feel again the grip of hell." And Zun whirled, flapping her immense sleeves, and slipped from the room, belching silently. She hoped that the pungent petals she had previously eaten would have their effect.

The Magistrate gaped in his empty room, stunned to inhale the fragrance of sweet osmanthus.

***

Lamps burned in the Consort's chambers. Zun watched Old Fong enter with a written message from the Magistrate, and exit quickly. Then the Consort herself swept out, in the direction of Ming Wen's quarters. But the lamps were not extinguished.

Zun waited a minute or so, and then crept into Lao's room. Bent over her desk was Ma Je, with a cup of tea and papers. Zun breathed deeply to calm herself. What would get Ma Je out of there? The Magistrate was one thing. Would *she* listen to a ghost? Slowly Zun fished out a vial from the green purse. Her big sleeve flapped, sending a tiny waft of air in Ma Je's direction.

Ma Je looked up from her reading, and surveyed the room, her hand on her teacup. She was about to take a sip. Here was Zun's chance.

She circled the perimeter of the room, her body below Ma Je's sight, until she reached the lamp near Lao's desk. She kicked her foot near the lamp, making the light flicker. Ma Je's eyes followed the movement, and in that instant Zun doubled back to drop a few grains of powder into Ma Je's tea.

But instead of sipping, Ma Je snorted, as if to make a mental note to harangue the maids about lamp-trimming. Zun crouched under the desk, her face at Ma Je's sour-smelling feet. She wondered how long the Consort would spend with Ming Wen. The Consort was clever enough to find an excuse to cut her visit short. Zun heard brushstrokes. Ma Je was busy writing. When would she get thirsty?

Finally, Ma Je pushed her chair back from the desk and stretched her neck. She reached for her tea a little too fast and spilled some on her lap. Rouged cheeks puffed in frustration, but to Zun's great relief, she poured the rest of the tea down her throat.

And went right back to work. A minute passed. It didn't take the prison guards this long to fall asleep.

Ma Je picked her teeth with a fingernail. She crossed her feet and fished around inside her mouth with energy and purpose. Did she have some sort of sleep-medicine antidote? Did Zun give her enough of the white powder?

The sleep medicine is a liquid, not a powder. You gave her the wrong thing!

It was very unlikely Ma Je would sleep. Zun stayed crouched behind the desk. Several long minutes later, Ma Je reached for her right side. Then she pressed her hand there, just below her ribcage. Her liver! She must have an uncomfortable awareness of the liver. Ma Je hurried from the room.

Zun popped up and scanned the papers on Ma Je's desk. They were covered with figures. Lists of equipment, dates, weights, and amounts of money: fabrics, wine, meat, eggs, vegetables. It looked like the household accounts. She ran to the Consort's desk. It was clear and neat. The drawers underneath contained only supplies – paper and ink. On top was a row of carved jade seals.

Zun whirled her head around the room. Nothing. There was a door probably leading to Lao's dressing room. Zun walked in and saw rows and rows of gowns. But at the end was another door. This door led to a completely dark room. Zun brought a lamp from the main room. The walls were covered with drawers. And inside each drawer were papers. Hundreds of pounds of papers, more papers than she could read in a month. She opened a drawer at random. In it were packets of papers tied together with string. Some were in envelopes with labels. They were tax records for Xiang village. Zun checked the labels on the front of each drawer. She scanned all the drawers and opened the one labeled "Water."

This one was interesting. There were reports from Engineer Shen, some of them dating back ten years. What was Lao doing with these documents? Didn't they belong to the office of the Magistrate?

She looked at more drawers and found one labeled "Armaments". Inside was a stack of documents labeled "Pang". They referred to shipments of metal. The foundry! Lao corresponded with Pang the foundry owner. Zun pondered what she should do with this information. If she took it, Lao would probably notice.

Zun searched for anything labeled "Wang" or "Hing," but nothing mentioned Wang Fei or Hing village.

Then she spotted a drawer marked "Tien Zi Wei". She racked her brain. It was a familiar name – who was it? She opened the drawer and found packets of letters. The letters from Tien Zi Wei had the Imperial Seal. He was the Governor! She found two recent letters bound together. The first was clearly a copy of a letter sent to the Governor, for it was not sealed.

Honored Governor:

The winds of autumn have brought us many blessings this year, and in return we seek to expand our forces. We would like to offer the Honored Governor a stake in our cannon factory, at no risk to you. The factory could make several thousand cannons a year, with iron from Chou Fu.

*We await the Honored Governor's considered reply.
With Subservient Greetings,*

Magistrate Jiang

The attached reply from the Governor was genuine, with the Governor's state seals. Zun slipped a stack of correspondence into her pocket. She crept back through the clothing closet and looked once more at Lao's desk. On a whim, she examined the seals. The first one she picked up, in plain sight on top of the desk, did not bear the character Lao. Instead, it said Jiang. It was the Magistrate's official seal. The doorknob clicked. Either Ma Je or the Consort was back.

Zun put the Magistrate's seal in her pocket and melted to the side of the room. Ma Je returned with a bowl of herbal soup. She sat down to the household accounts and slurped, still hugging her right side. Zun slid through the door behind Ma Je during an especially long and loud slurp.

In a dark alcove, she reviewed what she had learned. One, the Magistrate could not be bothered with official documents in his room. Two, Consort Lao had a secret room full of official documents. She had correspondence between the Magistrate and the next higher official, the Governor, and she had one of the Magistrate's seals, with which she could forge his letters. Did the Magistrate even know about the correspondence with the Governor in his name? She could find out.

Zun hastened to the Magistrate's chambers, hoping she would not run into old Fong. Several times she passed other servants and jumped, rolled, or dived to hide. If she passed Hu Laoban she'd be in big trouble. When she reached the Magistrate's quarters, she was in luck. She tried the knob, and it turned. She crept in.

The room was dark and smelled of burning charcoal. The Magistrate was asleep in his high bed, heated by braziers underneath. "Magistrate Jiang," said Zun in a deep voice. His eyes popped open and peered into the dimness.

"Who is there? Is that the Lady?"

"It is I, the Lady Under the Osmanthus," she said.

"I've done as you asked! Ming Wen has already begun to learn."

Zun made a dramatic rustle of her big white sleeves, and tossed the letters onto the Magistrate's bed. She handed him his spectacles.

"Tell me what you know of these letters!" She said.

He read them, and confusion spread on his face. "This letter appears to be from me," he said, 'but I did not write it. I have not seen this letter from the Governor. All the Governor's letters must come to me! Where did you get these?"

"Consort Lao has written letters in your name. It means that the Consort violates her rank in this household, even more than your daughter. Now my spirit can never rest!"

"Calm down, calm down, Lady Osmanthus. Maybe I asked her to write the letters. She is so helpful, you know, so refined. I will speak to her."

He didn't even care that the Consort forged his correspondence? What kind of official was he?

"The Lords of Hell will not stand for – "

The Magistrate scanned a letter from the Governor and shook it furiously. "This is … wait – "

"It is not enough to speak to her – " Zun intoned.

"So *that* is why!" he cried. "For years, for *years* I have been trying to leave this festering swamp-city and return to Beijing. And I could have left seven years ago. Someone used my seal and denied my transfer in my name!"

Zun threw his seal onto the bed. "This comes straight from Consort Lao's desk."

"The Consort has my seal! Lady Osmanthus, what must I do?"

"Imprison her, immediately!"

"Oh, Lady, anything but that. I'll hold the seal myself. No more mischief!"

"The winds of Hell will scream at you," intoned Zun. "And you'll never ever go back to Beijing."

"I can't believe she kept me in this wasteland. *No one here loves poetry!*"

23. Reunion

Zun hid in the gardenia bushes in the Magistrate's courtyard. She saw him put on his slippers and hobble from his private chamber. Fong met him in the hallway.

"Fong, Fong! Tell the Chief Constable and the General to meet me in the Tribunal office. I have very important news."

Zun followed the Magistrate to the entrance of the Tribunal office. The Chief Constable arrived, looking alert due to the lateness of the hour. When the General strode into the room, Fong closed the door.

She had to wait. The Chief Constable was the Magistrate's official second-in-command, and had been handpicked right at the start. Fong was a long-time servant. It wouldn't take long for the Magistrate to convince them to arrest Consort Lao.

The Magistrate stormed out the door waving the Governor's letters. "I said take her to the dungeon immediately!"

The General took his arm and twisted it behind his back.

Zun felt her plan wither as the Chief Constable emerged carrying leg irons, and beckoned to old Fong to help him put them on the Magistrate.

"I must follow Imperial Orders," said the General. "And I regret to inform your Honor that you must follow me to the dungeon."

"You have Imperial Orders to do this? Where's your proof?" shouted the Magistrate.

"Do you not know?" jeered the General. "I thought the gifted Magistrate Jiang knew all that passes in his Tribunal."

The Chief Constable glanced downward and made a little grimace.

Servants' heads popped into the courtyard, and as soon as they saw what was happening, popped back out.

The Magistrate stared at Fong as he passed, but Fong kept his eyes on the floor, as he had been trained to do. The Magistrate straightened himself and walked.

"When the Governor hears the true version of these proceedings, you will all be punished," he said.

Zun was close enough to Fong to hear him mutter.

"My nightmare," he said, 'is over."

The words sank in. The Magistrate was now a prisoner. He'd never be of any help to her. What could she do now? Was all that dressing up as a ghost a wasted effort? No. She knew who her real enemy was: the Consort. The one thing she had to do was rescue Ma. No more side paths and Spring Festivals. She had to find Ma and escape.

But where was Ma? She wasn't in the prison. *Think*. The one mystery in the compound was the windowless building. *I'll just go back there.*

Zun walked along the same path where she had followed the nickel-plated machine parts. The windowless building was dark. But in the night air, smells carried. From the windowless building came the smells of metal and leather and grease. Smells that Zun knew.

She watched. Eventually a man came from the direction of the kitchen. He carried a torch and a tray with tea. He was going to go inside! Zun sprang to her feet and followed him.

The man knocked on the door to the windowless building, and it opened. As he went inside, Zun slipped her foot in the crack. She saw the light from the man's torch recede. No one checked the door. She stepped in to the dark hallway. She could see the yellow cracks of a door to a lighted room ahead.

She crept to the door. The scent of familiar smells grew: metal and wood cuttings, paints, oils. She was able to peek through the crack of the door.

To Zun's astonishment, it opened to an immense high-ceilinged room full of strange bicycles in various states of construction. Huge bicycles, with thick wheels, and machines attached to the top tube. Engines? Motor bicycles? On the heavy handlebars of the more completed ones were cruel barbs and tubes. Harpoons and guns.

And in the voluminous space above the bicycles, in a metal cage hanging by chains from the ceiling, was Ma.

Her right arm was still in a bandage and her face was pushed against the bars of the cage, peering down at something.

Zun couldn't see the full room. As far as she could tell, no one was watching the door. She slid it open six inches, and put her head in. The tea servant had set a teapot on a bench. An armed guard was sipping some of the beverage. But that was not where Ma was looking. Zun couldn't see what she was staring at, so she just kept looking at Ma. At last Ma's face turned and she saw Zun at the door. Her eyes rounded in absolute horror.

"Go!" Ma mouthed silently, and wagged her arm out the door. Zun couldn't move. Ma glanced frantically around, and calmed her face, and returned to staring where she was staring. She even smiled. Then she very sneakily gave one dark, urgent look at the door.

Zun recoiled. She understood. There was at least one guard in there. She had to think of how to get Ma out.

She couldn't do anything now, but she'd have to do something tomorrow. She went back to the servants' sleeping room and tried to sleep.

The first thing Zun noticed in the morning was that her green purse was gone. She had no idea where she'd left it. The Magistrate's room? The Consort's? What would happen if it were found?

Hu set her to work scrubbing some courtyard steps. Fan stopped by and ordered more pork buns.

"Get them for me, and then I have something to tell you," Fan said.

Zun had no idea what it could be, but hurried to finish the steps and find a way to the kitchen.

She brought the pork buns to Fan in the main courtyard, where men were hammering something made of wood.

"Here are the buns, Fan," said Zun. She realized she knew what the men were making.

"What is that?" Fan pointed.

"It's a Tiptoe Box," said Zun. She looked at the ground.

"What's the matter with you?" demanded Fan.

At that question from Fan, of all people, Zun began to cry.

"Nothing," Zun mumbled. She rubbed her face all over with her sleeve. "Listen, Fan. You make sure Jung cleans her teeth every morning and night. You, too. A small brush is best; go all around. But even if you don't have a brush, you can make little picks – "

"Oh, listen to you!" Fan sounded disgusted. "You talk as if *you're* going to go into that box."

Zun resumed sobbing.

"Well you're not! Don't be silly," snapped Fan. "Wipe your slimy face."

Zun wiped and took a deep breath.

"And," Fan continued, "I'm supposed to give you a message. There's this weird twisted guy. He wheezes and leans on one side. He says he knows you."

Zun frowned. She didn't know anyone like that. "Go on."

"He said to tell you he's sorry he made you wear a four-hundred-pound coat. And he kept saying four hundred pounds – per second. He made me repeat it. Four hundred pounds per second. What's a 'second'?"

What on earth? "Tell me who's this person – what does he look like? Where is he?" Zun gasped.

"He's this gross guy they have chained up in some big work room. I don't think they ever let him wash himself. You should tell *him* to clean his teeth! He's building a bunch of noisy two-wheeled carts for the army."

Zun sat on her heels and sucked air. It had to be him. There was no one else he could be. It all added up. He was the only person who could build those strange big bicycles. *Ba's alive!*

"Haaaaa!" Zun emitted a strange crowing sound, exhilarated and panic-stricken in equal measure.

Fan shrugged and walked away.

"Wait, Fan!" cried Zun. "Please!"

But Fan had gone.

Ba had the wits to send her a message that said he was alive. She must try to get out and save him and Ma. The boys could help her. Maybe they could do the same things they did to break into the prison, except she didn't have the green purse. So they couldn't put any guards to sleep. They'd have to figure out another way.

Four hundred pounds per second. That didn't make any sense. Fan must've gotten it wrong. But she had insisted. Zun imagined an angry little farrier pounding a hammer four hundred times a second. And then she realized what Ba's clue meant: four hundred *beats* per second! That was a sound. A tone.

She ran to the stables to find Han and Li.

They were excited to see her.

Han said, "Wang Zun, we're taking you to see someone. He says he'll only talk to you, the daughter of Wang Fei and Chen Ru Lin."

"What? Never mind about that! You'll never believe it, but – "

"He's the rebel leader! He says he has something to ask you. Only you."

"Too bad! Listen to me, my father is alive!"

"What, did you see him?"

"No. No, but I saw my mother. And he sent me a message, through a servant who knows me. It could only be from him. Listen to me: the Consort is building weapons. Weapons that only my father can build. He's alive, and I have to get him and my mother out of here."

"Hmm. He must be heavily guarded," said Han.

"You'll help me, of course," said Zun.

"We'll use the sleep potion," said Li.

"I lost it. We'll have to find another way."

Li paced and pulled a tendril of his long glossy hair. "Wang Zun, you should see that rebel leader."

"Waste of time!"

"Think about it. Without the sleep potion, we need distractions to rescue your parents. Maybe the rebels can help us."

"All right, all right, then let's go!" Li made sense, but Zun felt impatient enough to burst.

She followed the boys to a remote workroom in the stable. A man waited there. He looked up at Zun and she recognized his purple scars. *The man we broke out of jail!*

"Wang Zun," he said. "Did you know your father is alive?"

"You could've told me that before," she said.

"I only found out recently," he said. "Listen, you have to make him stop!"

"Stop what?"

"Stop building weapons for the Consort!"

Zun crossed her arms on her chest. "He's a prisoner. He's being forced to do it. The things he's building are uglier than you can imagine. Anyway if he's not even finished, what does it matter?"

"The men in the army are ready to rebel," he said.

"Then rebel tonight! Before he finishes," said Zun.

"But they know the Consort has a huge cache of weapons. Explosives, cannons, and some kind of secret deadly weapon that only a few selected men will operate – the weapon built by your father. You must tell him to stop."

The man made no sense to Zun. The rebels should fight now if they wanted to win. Two lines from the poem that the Consort had given to Ma popped into her head:

What good is the heart of a hero
Beneath this woman's dress?

Words from the Consort, words of anguish. Maybe that's what the Consort intended – for Ma and Zun to read those words and dive down into despair. Zun snorted in automatic revolt. Dress or no dress, a hero's still a hero. And thinking of the Consort, Zun felt sure of one thing. Dress or no dress, a villain's still a villain.

"How many rebels are in the army?" she asked.

"The whole army is about five hundred. And probably three hundred are rebels," said the scarred man.

"Then what's the problem? Can't three hundred beat two hundred?"

The scarred man sighed. "You don't understand. These men have all lost something, or someone. Their homes were burned, or their family was beaten. They are with us against the Consort, but afraid."

"If we destroy the weapons tonight," she leaned toward the man, "would the men fight the Consort? This very night?"

The man sneezed in reply, and got a nosebleed. He left without giving Zun a definite answer.

24. The Invisible Squirrel Strikes

Zun walked in on Fan and Jung in the kitchen. They fed the fire in the stove for the hot water kettles.

As soon as Fan saw Zun, she smirked.

"I hear you're a rebel – "

Jung whacked her on the arm. "Shut up! Shut up, you idiot!"

Fan was so shocked she just rubbed her arm.

Zun grabbed Jung's hand and squeezed it. "I need to warn you – "

"I'm not going to get a flogging because of a rebel," said Fan, turning to go.

"If you get a toothache, is the Lady going to help you? Or Hu?" Jung demanded.

Fan stopped, but kept her back to Zun and Jung.

"Jung, the sleeping chamber is going to burn tonight," said Zun. "But you'll be all right; I'm going to let you all out. And I need sugar and saltpeter, and fresh pork blood."

Fan turned around. "Just what do you mean?"

"I mean the rebels are going to attack. If you want to stay alive tonight, listen to me."

"Let's check the pickling shelves." Jung pointed at a row of shelves across the room.

Zun tasted the powders in the jars and soon hit upon the salt-sour taste of saltpeter. She mixed it with granulated sugar and poured the mixture into four porcelain tumblers, and planted twine for fuses on top. She covered the tumblers with cloth bound with more twine.

Li tapped her on the shoulder. Zun gasped.

"Don't do that! Can't you see what I'm doing?" she said.

Jung and Fan stared at Han and Li who had come in.

Fan nudged Jung. "Is that a boy?" She was looking at Li. "Look at his hair."

Both she and Jung stared at Li's long glossy front hair. They each smoothed their own hair away from their faces.

"Did you get the hand bombs and fuses?" asked Zun.

Han and Li nodded.

Zun found two empty rice sacks and put the smoke bombs she had just made in one sack, the hand bombs and fuses in the other.

"Remember, Jung and Fan, go to bed as usual tonight. Put the rags in my bed so Hu thinks I'm there. I'll come for you!"

She nodded to the boys and they left the kitchen.

They walked as far west inside the Magistrate's house as they could, to approach the barracks without being sighted by the soldiers. They popped out into the main courtyard near the northwest corner.

The barracks had two main doors. Sentries paced in front of the building. All they had to do was block the two main doors, and the sleeping soldiers would be trapped inside. Zun pointed to a tree that overhung the entrance, and the boys climbed up. They offered her a hand and she clambered onto a limb.

"Now we wait," she whispered.

She had to be sure that the servants were locked in the sleeping chamber. When it was time, she nodded to the boys.

As soon as the sentries paced away from the door, Zun attached a hand bomb to a branch overhanging the barracks entrance.

"What are you doing?" Li whispered.

"I'm going to blow off this branch and block the barrack door," said Zun.

"You can't destroy this tree," he said.

"What, are you crazy! We don't have time to worry about trees. Better that than collapse the whole roof on their heads," Zun replied.

"You don't have to," Li murmured, staring at the roof of the barracks. "Look at the roofline. There's an entryway. If Han and I go up and weaken the boundary, only that part of the roof will fall down – it'll block the entryway. You set the explosive at the base of the column holding it up."

Zun nodded. "But what about the noise? If you kick or hack at the roof, won't it make too much noise?"

Li frowned.

"Timing," said Zun. "We have to time it so you kick on it, and then just five counts later the bombs explode. You have to get out of the way quickly."

"Well, if my plan works, the roof will hold and we'll be safe."

Again they waited for the sentries to pace away, and Zun climbed down. She hurried to the base of the first column to set her charge. She tied it to the column and fed out the line. She heard Li and Han skitter up the roof. She ran to the other door, on the other side of the building, and stretched out a longer piece of fuse. She saw the boys wave their arms against the sky. They were ready. She crouched behind a bush and lit both fuses with a match.

The orange sparks snaked towards the column, leaving a smoky tang in the air. She heard Li and Han kick methodically at the roof. A few men grunted inside at the disturbance.

Sentries approached the first door, chatting. "If they make us work extra at night they should at least give us another hot meal."

"You said it. Is that something on the roof?"

"Stupid squirrel. Never get a good night's rest."

"That's bigger than a squirrel."

"Nah, the squirrels here are monsters. Did you see Jing's finger? Almost bitten off, and now it's black. That was a squirrel."

The lit fuse was completely visible in the path. Zun had to do something.

"No, look! That's not – ooh!"

Zun had stuck her foot out and tripped them. They fell in a heap. The spark reached the first bomb and it went off.

"*Aiya*!" screamed the two sentries, covering their heads.

The column buckled and the front part of the roof fell. Then the second charge went off. Men inside the barracks yelled.

Zun and the boys rolled under the bushes.

A stream of sentries ran to the barracks.

Zun and the boys ran to the servants' quarters. Zun picked the lock and darted inside.

"Fan, Jung, girls! Come out!" she whispered.

Jung left the room last, carrying a pail of pork blood.

Han and Li went in to set another bomb.

Zun waved at them and headed for the Consort's chambers. *Four hundred beats per second.* That was Ba's message to her. She knew it could only refer to one thing, and that was the chime on the Consort's wall clock. It sounded a pure tone at exactly that frequency, four hundred beats per second. Zun knew because Ba had explained it to her when he tuned the clock. Ba needed that chime, and Zun had a feeling she knew why.

The chamber door was locked, but Zun took out her bamboo picks and wires. She opened the door and immediately ducked behind the wall to the left side.

Five three-bladed stars whizzed out and embedded themselves in the wooden wall opposite. Ma Je was inside. Zun didn't breathe. Ma Je didn't move outside the door, but waited too.

Silently, Zun took out a canister of sugar and saltpeter, lit the fuse, and rolled it inside the room.

At the sound of the match Ma Je threw more stars, and didn't see the rolling canister.

Zun heard a *poof* sound, and smelled smoke. Ma Je coughed but stayed inside.

At the sound of Ma Je's cough, Zun froze. Even though the clock was there, Ma Je still terrified her. Seconds ticked by.

Boom! Han and Li had set off a bomb in the servant's chamber. A second later Zun heard screams. Crouching low, she stepped into the room, and moved along the wall.

A few steps later Zun could hear the wall clock ticking. She reached for it, but a terrible pain shot through her arm. Ma Je had knocked her arm away as hard as she could. Zun kicked her away and Ma Je landed with a penetrating thud.

"Help! Help me!" cried a hoarse voice through the smoke.

Jiang Ming Wen came into the Consort's room, dressed in night robes and carrying her prized ginseng root. "What's happening?" she cried.

"Help me subdue this rebel, you fool!" screamed Ma Je from the floor.

"Fire!" someone screamed.

A girl ran past the Consort's room, her face dripping with blood. Pig's blood, as Zun knew. "The whole compound is afire!"

"Save the root, honored lady," said Zun to Ming Wen. "You must save the root!"

Ming Wen clutched the ginseng root to her chest and ran after the blood-streaked servant.

Zun grabbed the Consort's clock and sped from the room. She slammed the door on Ma Je and shoved a huge vase against it. She piled up whatever she could: a carved end table, a painting, a jade relief, a porcelain sage. She hoped it would hold up Ma Je and the Consort for a while.

She tucked the clock under her arm and ran to the windowless building where Ma and Ba were kept.

The plan was working. The compound was in an uproar and no one paid any attention to her. The servants ran for their lives, spooked by the explosions and the screaming girls covered with blood.

But when she reached the courtyard of the windowless building she came to a dead stop. The guards were still there, on patrol. Nothing had moved them from their post. A couple of additional guards were there too. She had no idea how she would get in.

25. Smoked Pork With Bamboo Shoots

Zun found the Magistrate walking before the General on the path to the windowless building.

"Thank you for releasing me, General. You've taken upon yourself the restoration of the Confucian ideal. I would now appreciate a hot bath. The stench of that prison cell is unfit for men of learning."

The General pushed the Magistrate into the courtyard. He led the Magistrate to a spot on the ground several yards from the windowless building. "On your knees, old man," he said.

The Magistrate howled when his knees hit the cold gravel of the courtyard.

"Hands behind your head!" said the General, and took out his sword.

Zun felt the slightest swish beside her. Han and Li were next to her, staring across the courtyard.

"Wait!" called a commanding female voice. Ma Je's. She and the Consort walked over to the General and spoke to him. Zun couldn't hear what they were saying, but the General sent a soldier inside the windowless building.

Two men emerged with a small woman in the middle. A one-armed woman. Zun held her breath.

"Wang Zun! Rebels!" Ma Je's big voice rang out. "Surrender immediately or watch Chen Ru Lin be killed!"

The men pushed Ma to kneel down on the cold courtyard gravel beside the Magistrate.

Zun touched Han and Li's arms and pulled them back. All they could see of one another were dark shadows against the dimness. She pointed to the windowless building, to herself, and back to the building.

The boys nodded. She had to get there somehow.

She held up her last two smoke bombs. She pointed from a smoke bomb to the courtyard.

Li took her hand, touched it to a smoke bomb, and held up a hand. With his other hand, he walked two fingers towards the place in the courtyard where Ma and the Magistrate kneeled. Then he dragged the smoke bomb out.

Zun understood. Li would attack and show himself first. Then she had to throw the first smoke bomb.

There were at least six armed soldiers in the courtyard, and the General, and Ma Je. They were big and scary, and for a horrible moment Zun could not move. Her only chance was to find the trapdoor in the ground, open it, and get into the windowless building. If the boys couldn't fight off all those people in the courtyard, she would never make it. But they had no other option. She imagined Li dispersing the soldiers like pigeons. She imagined herself running right past them.

Han and Li silently did rock-paper-scissors. Li won, and grinned.

But before he could do anything, Han ran into the courtyard with his pitchfork.

At first the men didn't even see him. There was a shout, and they threw knives at him. Han wheeled and dodged, and managed to reach a soldier and fight him. Other soldiers struggled to aim their guns.

Li lit a match, and then the smoke bomb. Zun rolled it towards Ma and the Magistrate.

With a shout, Li brandished his staff and ran toward the soldiers.

With shaking hands Zun lit the second smoke bomb and rolled it into the courtyard. The smoke plumed and rolled, but still didn't cover the courtyard. Zun stood up.

"Squeeee!" A terrible scream seared Zun's ears, and a black-and-white barrel shot through the courtyard, bowling over several soldiers. Pig-Pig! Not far behind him, a small clean shadow of a man dipped into the smoke surrounding Ma and the Magistrate. It had to be Shifu.

Zun could no longer watch. It was time for her to move. She ran across the courtyard hoping no one would notice her. She couldn't find the exact location of the trapdoor in the ground. She stamped her feet and listened for hollow sounds, but with the surrounding battle no one could hear her. All around Zun were horrible noises, of Pig-Pig squealing in rage, pieces of metal crashing together, and men yelling. She noticed the General fighting someone who carried two sticks.

"Pig-Pig!" she cried. "Pig-Pig!"

He bounded through the smoke to her.

She stamped her foot on the ground, and got down on her hands and knees. Pig-Pig sniffed at the ground, and went straight to a wooden panel. He had found it.

Its sides were flush with the ground, and there was no way for Zun to open it. She dug frantically at one edge. Pig-Pig gently nudged her until she rolled over.

Infuriated, she pushed back, but he had started digging. In a matter of seconds he freed the edge of the trapdoor from the surrounding dirt. Zun pried it up and jumped in. Pig-Pig didn't follow. He knew better than to jump into a black hole.

She slid several yards down a wooden slide to a black tunnel.

"Wang Zun!" She heard someone come down after her. She scrambled out of the way.

"It's me, Han. Let's go!" She heard the trapdoor snap shut above. "That's Li shutting the door. Hurry!"

There was only one way down the tunnel. A flight of stairs led up into the building. Zun opened a door into bright light. She was in the big laboratory again. Two big guards paced the aisles.

They shouted at the sight of Zun, and Han burst past her. He knocked over a bench and pinned one of them, and led the other on a chase around the room.

Zun searched the benches frantically. "Ba!" She called. "Ba!"

"Zun!" At last, his voice!

She ran to a corner of the laboratory and found him, chained to a wall. He was dirty, and his right shoulder was hiked up somehow, but it was Ba! She'd have gladly been a slave a thousand days longer for this moment. She threw herself into his arms.

He squeezed her hard. "Zun, Zun, what's happening outside? Where's your mother?"

"Ba, I brought the chime. The four hundred hertz chime. I got your message, Ba! It's a trigger, isn't it?"

"That's my girl! You've got a brain and a half! Who's this?"

Han had popped up behind Zun.

"Ba, this is Hing Han. You know, one of Shifu's babies!"

"No!" said Han. "I mean, I *was* a baby – "

"Hing Han – of course I remember! How you've grown! What a pleasure to see you. Now listen, both of you. Zun's guess is right. All these evil machines I built for the Consort are rigged up to explode at a sound of four hundred hertz. Help me set up this chime and amplify it. Eventually this whole building will come down. But tell me – is Ma safe?"

"She's out in the courtyard," said Zun. "They … they threatened to kill her unless I came out and the rebels surrendered."

"We have to end this now. We'll blow up this building and rescue your mother."

"How will we get you out, Ba?"

His chains were forged to the wall. There was no padlock.

"We'll worry about that later," said Ba. "Go on, get that big metal gong-shaped thing. Strap the chime on that table over there. Hurry!"

Zun did as he said, but didn't see how they'd break Ba's chain.

"Zun, hand me that screwdriver!"

Ba opened up the clock and freed the chime from the clock mechanism.

"Now, we need something to set off the chime repeatedly," said Ba.

"The motors on those big bicycles," said Zun. "Attach a transverse bar to the crankshaft to hit the chime. Use a couple of gears to make it hit at the right frequency."

"That's it again! You haven't forgotten a thing in these months!"

"As if I'd forget that!"

"Go get a motor!"

The motors were too heavy for Zun to lift by herself. Han helped her carry one to Ba's workbench, and they set up the chime.

"Now get out of here," said Ba. "I won't start it until you leave."

"No, Ba, we'll get you out first!" Zun screamed. She picked up a hammer and started smashing at the chain.

"It'll take too long, Zun-a. At any minute, the Consort could kill your mother. If we destroy this building, the Consort will lose her power and won't have a reason to keep your mother or you anymore. You and Hing Han must save yourselves and your mother."

"No Ba no," said Zun, and ran to one of the bicycles. "Han, help me!"

They wheeled the heavy motorized bicycle to Ba's chain and aimed its gun at it, and fired. There was a loud bang. The chain splintered but didn't break. They shot at it again and again. A piece of metal flew up and hit Ba on the head. His eyes rolled up and he fell to the ground. But the chain was broken.

"Han, get him out of here!" Zun shouted.

When Han had dragged Ba to the tunnel doorway, she started the motor for the chime. It was a small kerosene engine, and it started with a simple kick-starter. The chime went off about twice a second: *bong-bong! Bong-bong!*

But nothing happened. Zun felt her panic rise. Was it going to work? Should she change the motor frequency? She couldn't think past the horrible noise. Suddenly, with great relief, she heard an ominous creak. She began to run.

All through the laboratory, a vibration grew and grew. She reached the door to the tunnel just as the first explosion sounded, and slammed the door shut behind her. She ran down the black tunnel as another explosion hit, and then another. She stumbled right into Han and Ba at the bottom of the slide. She put her hands over her ears as countless explosions thundered above.

26. Red Pumpkins Ride Again

Zun rested her hands in her lap. She looked around the tiny dim kitchen with pleasure. It was hard to believe she was back in her apartment in the Fu building again, with Ma and Ba asleep in the next room. They needed a lot of rest. Ba's right lung had partially collapsed from his stab wound, and he'd never be as strong as he was. That was why he wheezed and his shoulders weren't straight anymore.

But they were alive. At the sound of the explosions in the windowless building, the rebel soldiers in the barracks had turned on the General. After securing Ma safely in the house, Shifu had caught Ma Je and the Consort and put them in the Magistrate's prison.

Li and the scarred man had organized some soldiers to dig open the trapdoor and rescue Zun, Han, and Ba from the tunnel.

Zun picked up her new green tunic from her lap and admired her handiwork. Along the bottom hem was a row of embroidered red pumpkins. She took off the jacket she had worn against the morning cold, and put on the new tunic.

Ba hobbled in. "Good morning, Zun-a! Is today the big day?"

"Today it is."

"On your way out, tell Shifu and the boys to come over for lunch. I have something to show them."

Shifu and the boys lived in the Fu building too, for now. Only time would tell if the evil nuns would reappear.

Zun put on her jacket and a plain black cap, and hopped on the Phoenix. She pedaled towards the Magistrate's house.

It was still early. As she rode through the city streets, it was as if nothing had happened. Like any morning, farmers entered the gates with vegetables, and thin trails of smoke rose from kitchen fires. People set up stands in the market. Bakers baked and blacksmiths hammered. Newspapers lined the shelves at teahouses, for Zhang Po had escaped the Tiptoe Box in time.

Yet everything inside the Magistrate's house had changed.

Jung and Fan slept in clean beds, personally inspected for insects by Shifu. The Magistrate sent many of the soldiers recently recruited by the Consort, such as the Fu brothers, home. Hei ran a free clinic beside the farrier's forge.

Even Ming Wen had new duties. She trained the Magistrate's constables in the principles of muscle growth.

Zun rode to the compound and breezed past the sentries at the gate. He was there, in the main courtyard, waiting. Just as the first day she had seen him, he was a small, blinking, owl-faced man, but this time he was alone. He had no retinue of vermillion-clad footmen, no scurrying manservant. His plain, heavy winter robe seemed to drift in the winter breeze.

Zun braked the Phoenix to a stop. Ba had fixed it to fit her. He had lowered the main seat and added a second seat and footrests behind, for a passenger. Ba was too weak to ride the bicycle anymore, but Zun could.

"Greetings, Wang Zun," the Magistrate said. "I've considered the bicycle factory proposal fully, and have come to the conclusion that it is a viable investment for the county, and thus there is no need for this morning outing. In view of the bitter wind, let us seal our agreement over tea in my chambers."

Zun felt as if Ming Wen's ginseng root was stuck in her throat. In a way the old man was right – the main thing was that he had agreed to build the bicycle factory. But the empty seat on the back of the Phoenix reproached her. Ba couldn't even ride it. The Magistrate was old, but whole.

"You agreed to come," she said.

"Surely I've done enough? Your mother runs the court; your father will have the factory! What more do you want?"

"Can you give my mother a new arm? Or my father a lung?" Zun said.

The Magistrate's face became as grey as the courtyard gravel.

"Just straddle that seat," she said, and held the bicycle steady.

The Magistrate had to lift his robe to get his leg over the seat. His bony ankles were bare above his thick felted shoes.

She straddled the bicycle and looked back at the old man.

"You must hang on to my jacket," said Zun. When they got back to the road, it was easier, although the road had deep ruts from all the carts, and the ruts were cold and hard.

"Stop, please. This is the most bumpy and uncomfortable ride in the world. My hands are cold," said the Magistrate.

"Wrap them in your sleeves!"

"My buttocks ache severely."

They came to a small hill and Zun felt the full weight of the Magistrate.

"You'll never make it up this hill. Let me down!"

But Zun wasn't going to let a little hill stop her.

They crested the hill as the sun broke through the morning cloud.

She felt the old man's hands twist the loose cloth of her grey robe, and coasted down the hill. The rising sun sent a beam of winter gold over the low mists ahead. The bicycle rolled faster and faster and it was all she could do to avoid holes and ruts.

"I'm wobbling!" the Magistrate cried. "I'm so cold! I'll fall!"

"Hold on to me!" she yelled. "Do it!"

His hands clapped around her waist. Her eyes streamed in the breeze as they picked up speed. The old man's hands gripped tighter. They careened along the flat stretch at the bottom of the hill. A roosting owl flapped away on big silent wings as they approached.

She pushed through the bottom of a rounded valley. Winter's hand lay on everything: the crunch of the wheels over frozen puddles, the cold that clenched her wrists and ankles, and the wilderness of frost all around them. And yet – despite the void and the cold, the absence of leaf and the silence – every breath she took as they sliced through the air felt like life itself. *How*, she wondered, *could this great bowl of frozen winter air be so alive?*

She was startled by a loud bleating noise in her left ear.

"*A thousaaaaand mountains: no birds in fliiiight.*"

It was the Magistrate! He was singing.

*"A thousand mountains: no birds in flight.
Countless trails, not a single footfall.
A lone boat, in straw raincoat and bamboo hat, an old man
Fishes in the frigid river snow."*

He sang the River Snow poem by Liu Zong Yuan. Zun was so shocked she could only listen.

"I think, after all this time," the Magistrate shouted, "I get it!" He sang it again. He was loud, but the song lit a fire in Zun's feet. She pedaled and pedaled, on into the morning.

ACKNOWLEDGMENTS

The author thanks:

Susan Cabael
Patricia Campbell
Jeannette Cheng
Thida Cornes
Ariane Erickson
Todd Erickson
Uma Krishnaswami
Oi Ha Lam
Tischa Lamprecht
Jay Lehmann
Alan Liu
Ava Liu
Miranda Liu
Megan Wagner Lloyd
Doug Marshall
Layne Sheppard Salter
Rebecca Sladek
Eileen Tse
Maya Venkatraman

For insight, feedback and friendship along the way.

ABOUT THE AUTHOR

Marjorie Sayer was born in Hong Kong to parents of Chinese, English, Persian, and Indian descent. She is happiest reading, writing, playing music or doing mathematics. She lives in California with her husband and two daughters.

CPSIA information can be obtained at www.ICGtesting.com
Printed in the USA
LVOW04s0003170914

404336LV00030B/1193/P